PUFFIN BOOKS

THE SECRET PASSAGE

'We're burglars, aren't we?' Ben asked, as John struggled to unlock the door from the cellar into the empty house.

'Not really,' said Mary fiercely. 'I mean we're not going to steal anything. We can't be doing any *harm*.'

But to judge by John's desperate efforts, it didn't look as if they were going to get into the house anyway. It had been tremendously exciting to find the passage from Aunt Mabel's cellar and think that now they'd really be able to see inside the mysteriously deserted house next door. Exploring it would have taken their minds off the whole tragic business of their mother's death, the disappearance of their father, and being dumped on gruff Aunt Mabel, but now they were facing defeat.

Then Ben suddenly called, 'But the door's not locked at all!' And sure enough, there was a crack of light round the sides. The door of the empty house wasn't locked any more, but *who* had let them in?

There is mystery after mystery as this story unfolds, and plenty of interesting characterization too, as the children get to know Aunt Mabel and her two eccentric lodgers, not to mention their enigmatic friend Victoria, who is so strangely ungrateful for all their efforts to stop her from starving.

The Secret Passage was the first of Nina Bawden's children's books, and it's an excellent story of three lonely children who have a real adventure.

Nina Bawden was born in London, educated at the local grammar school and then at Oxford. She has been a farm hand, a postwoman, and a town planner; she started to write while she was at school and had her first novel published in 1952. She is married, has two sons and a daughter and lives in London.

Other books by Nina Bawden

CARRIE'S WAR
THE FINDING
A HANDFUL OF THIEVES
KEPT IN THE DARK
ON THE RUN
THE PEPPERMINT PIG
REBEL ON A ROCK
THE ROBBERS
THE RUNAWAY SUMMER
SQUIB
THE WHITE HORSE GANG
THE WITCH'S DAUGHTER

Nina Bawden

The Secret Passage

*

PUFFIN BOOKS

PUFFIN BOOKS

Penguin Books Ltd, 27 Wrights Lane, London W8 5TZ (Publishing and Editorial)
and Harmondsworth, Middlesex, England (Distribution and Warehouse)
Viking Penguin Inc., 40 West 23rd Street, New York, New York 10010, USA
Penguin Books Australia Ltd, Ringwood, Victoria, Australia
Penguin Books Canada Ltd, 2801 John Street, Markham, Ontario, Canada L3R 1B4
Penguin Books (NZ) Ltd, 182–190 Wairau Road, Auckland 10, New Zealand

First published by Victor Gollancz Ltd 1963
Published by Pan Books Ltd 1972
Published (opening chapters shortened) in Puffin Books 1979
Reprinted 1980, 1981, 1982, 1983, 1984, 1986, 1988

Made and printed in Great Britain by
Richard Clay Ltd, Bungay, Suffolk
Set in Linotype Granjon

For Nicholas, Robert and Perdita

CONTENTS

1. 'England Must be a Very Small Place'

When John and Mary and Ben Mallory first saw their Aunt Mabel they thought she looked very disagreeable. She was tall and thin with a long, thin face and grey hair insecurely fastened in a straggly bun at the back of her neck. Whenever she turned her head, a little shower of hairpins fell out. When she met the children at London Airport, she was wearing a faded brown coat and stockings that wrinkled on her skinny legs as if they had been intended for a much fatter person.

John thought she probably looked like that, so shabby and cross, because she was a widow. His father had told him that her husband, Mr Haggard, had been drowned at sea. But Ben thought it must be because she lived in England. He had lived in Africa all his life; this was his first visit to England and he had decided, almost as soon as he got off the plane, that he didn't like it. How horrible it was, not at all like Africa – so cold and grey and sunless. No wonder Aunt Mabel looked pinched and hunched-up and pale.

Her voice sounded disagreeable too. The very first thing she said to them was, 'Here you are! I thought you were never coming. Your plane is two hours late.'

It did not occur to the children that she had been worried. They thought she was simply angry.

'I'm sorry,' Mary said timidly. There was a hard, uncomfortable lump in her throat and she had a funny, fluttery feeling in her stomach – sick and hungry at the same time. They were coming to live here, with Aunt Mabel because their mother had died of pneumonia and their father was ill. Mrs Epsom, the district commissioner's wife, who had looked after the children when their mother went to the hospital, had told them he had had a nervous breakdown. Mary had not understood what that meant; she only knew that her father had seemed very silent and strange when he had put them on the plane in Nairobi. She had cried and clung to him and begged him to let her stay, but he had kissed her and told her to be a brave girl and give his love to Aunt Mabel. So although it was exciting to come to England – as exciting as visiting a foreign country – it had been a sad journey too. All the long hours in the plane Mary had felt the sad part and the exciting part churning around inside her. And now that she had seen Aunt Mabel she felt she wanted to cry.

'Oh – it's not your fault,' Aunt Mabel said. She looked at Mary and then bent to kiss her cheek. It was a clumsy little peck as if she was not really used to kissing people. She shook hands with John and said, 'I expect all grown-ups tell you that you've grown. As far as I'm concerned, you really have. You were fifteen months old when I last saw you. That was just before you went out to Kenya.'

'I'm afraid I don't remember you,' John said very politely. 'But I was very young and it was a long time ago. I'm twelve now and Mary's eleven. Ben's only seven, but he's big for his age.'

'He certainly is,' Aunt Mabel said. She glanced rather nervously at Ben, who was glaring at her in the fierce way he had when he was wondering what people were like. Aunt Mabel thought he looked more like an African boy than an English one, with his dark, sunburnt skin and dark eyes. She said, 'You need a hair-cut.'

It wasn't a very encouraging remark, but Ben grinned at her and took her hand as they went out to the airport bus.

John and Mary were quiet in the bus. They felt that their aunt was not very pleased to see them. But Ben bounced and wriggled on the seat, looking out of the window and squealing with excitement. He had never seen so many houses and roads and cars before.

'England must be a very small place,' he said suddenly.

'What a funny thing to say,' Aunt Mabel said. It didn't sound as if she thought it was funny, her voice was slightly annoyed, but after a minute she smiled at Ben just the same. It is difficult not to smile at someone who expects you to smile at him. She didn't understand what he meant, but John and Mary did. The hundreds and hundreds of houses were all so small and cramped together that it looked as if there couldn't be enough space for people to live comfortably.

'Wherever do all the children play?' Ben said in an astonished voice.

Aunt Mabel glanced out of the windows. 'In the gardens, if they're lucky enough to have them. If not, in the streets or the parks.'

'But there's no room,' Ben said. 'Round our house there was miles and miles and miles.'

Their farm, in Kenya, was near a river at the foot of a mountain. From the bungalow they could see snow-capped peaks, a range of lower, blue-coloured hills, and the African village on the ridge across the valley – a group of conical-shaped straw huts that steamed sometimes in the damp weather as if they were on fire. There were no dangerous snakes, and though there were lions and elephants and rhinos, they hid deep in the forests, high up the mountains, so John and Mary and Ben had been free to go wherever they liked. The blue hills, the wide, beautiful valley, had been their playground.

'Well, there's no room here,' Aunt Mabel said shortly. 'Certainly not in the towns, and in the country there are fields full of crops and you aren't allowed to play in those, let me tell you.'

Ben wrinkled his nose. 'It sounds horrid,' he said.

John and Mary looked at each other. It did sound depressing and it looked depressing too. The sky was lead grey and seemed to press down low over the little houses and the crowded streets and the hurrying people. It was all very flat, there were no hills and only a few dead-looking trees – John thought they were dead until he remembered that in England the trees lost their green leaves in winter. Their bus swept into London over the Hammersmith Flyover.

'Look!' shouted Ben, kneeling up on his seat. 'The cars are going underneath. We're up in the air.'

John and Mary might have been excited by this too if they had not been so cold. Even Aunt Mabel, who didn't seem inclined to notice things about people, saw that they were cold. When they got out of the bus and were waiting for a taxi to take them to the railway station, she turned Mary's collar up round her neck and said, 'That coat isn't warm enough. Your blood must have got thin with being in Africa.'

'Mrs Epsom said you would get us some warm clothes,' John said.

'She said you would probably buy us some toys too,' Ben added with a happy grin. In Africa he had had very few toys of the kind English children play with. He had had a stone called William that he painted faces on and dressed up in bits of his mother's old dresses and a chameleon called Balthazar, who had a loosely fitting skin like a pair of very baggy trousers and two bright pinpoint eyes that swivelled round to watch you when you moved, as if they were on ball bearings. Mrs Epsom had told him Aunt Mabel would buy him toys, to comfort him when he realized he would have to leave Balthazar behind.

'Oh, she did, did she?' Aunt Mabel said. She didn't say anything else until they were sitting in the train and eating the ham sandwiches she produced out of a brown carrier bag. While they ate she watched them thoughtfully and rather anxiously with her sharp brown eyes. She was thinking of the letter Mrs Epsom had written to her.

I imagine that their father will eventually make some financial arrangement for the children, but at the moment he is in no state to do so. He is quite broken up by his wife's death and we are afraid that unless he recovers soon the farm will go to rack and ruin. He talks of selling the farm, but it is unlikely he will find a buyer in the present political situation. He seems to have no money in the bank. We think he has always lived beyond his income. The children seem always to have had everything they want. You will find them very spoiled as well as uneducated. Their mother taught them at home instead of sending them to school. My husband has advanced the money for their fares and a few clothes. I have asked Mr Mallory over and over again if you can afford to support the children, but all he says is: There is no one else ...

Aunt Mabel said in a brusque voice, 'You may as well know – I can't afford to buy you a lot of clothes and toys and things.'

They looked at her in surprise and she went on in an odd, almost indignant, way, 'Mrs Epsom says you've been used to having everything you want. I think we'd better get it straight from the beginning. You'll not go without anything you really need, but there's no money for frills. I hope you'll understand that.'

'Yes, Aunt Mabel,' Mary said, though she didn't really understand at all. She supposed they always had had everything they wanted, but it had never seemed to cost much money. After all, there were so few shops where they lived, in Africa, that it would have been difficult to spend a lot of money. She wondered if Aunt Mabel was really poor and if they would all have to live in a mud hut, but she didn't like to ask her.

Ben wasn't so tactful. He said, looking bright and interested, 'Are you a beggar, then?'

Aunt Mabel's face went very red. 'Certainly not.'

John said quickly, 'He didn't mean to be rude. He just wanted to know if you were really poor like some of the Africans are. Some of their children have big swollen stomachs that stick right out because they're starving.'

'Oh,' said Aunt Mabel. 'Oh – I see.' She said, to Ben, 'I'm not poor, not in that way. But I keep a boarding-house and if it's a bad season, I don't make very much money. When it rains a lot, no one wants to come to the sea, and they cancel their bookings.'

The children looked at her blankly.

'What is a boarding-house?' Ben said.

'It's a place people go to for holidays. It's my house, you see, and they pay me to come and be guests in it. I've only got two guests now because it's winter. Mr Agnew and Miss Pin. Mr Agnew is a sculptor – he's very busy all the time, and you must be sure and not bother him. Miss Pin is – is a little peculiar.' She gave a little sigh. 'Just now, there isn't anyone else.'

Mary said, 'Is it the same house that you and Mother lived in, when you were girls?'

'No. That's the house next door. It's a big place – when my husband died it was too big for me to keep up. So I sold it to a man who took a fancy to it; he wanted it for summers, he said – he had more money than sense, if you ask me – and now he's old and ill and it's shut up mostly. It's a pity, it's a nice old place with a huge garden and lots of rambling rooms. And attics. We used to play up in the attics – you can see the sea from some of the windows, and there was an old brass bedstead that we used to play on. We used to tie string to the posts and pretend we were driving a horse and cart. I wonder if it's still there – I left a lot of stuff behind when I left and as far as I know he never turned anything out.'

Aunt Mabel smiled and her face was soft and much gentler, suddenly, as if she were remembering a very happy time.

Mary said, 'What was our mother like, when she was a little girl?' Her eyes were very bright and she was breathing very fast. John and Ben looked at her and then down at their feet. It was the first time any of them had spoken about their mother since the dreadful morning Mrs Epsom had come into their room and told them that they would never see her again. Mary's question made them feel very lost and strange.

Aunt Mabel caught her breath. 'She was very pretty. Very pretty and gay.' She looked at John and Ben, sitting still and silent as wax images and then she looked at Mary as if she were really seeing her for the first time. She said in a low voice, 'She looked a little bit like you . . .'

The train stopped. A large notice on the platform said HENSTABLE, and outside the Waiting Room there was a coloured poster of a girl in a bathing costume, sitting by a bright, blue sea. The poster said, Sunny Henstable Welcomes You.

They didn't feel very welcomed, though. It was dark and

cold and the wind sliced through their thin clothes like a sharp knife.

'It must be like the North Pole,' said Ben.

They climbed into a taxi and drove away from the twinkling lights of the station, into the dark town. The houses all seemed very tall and narrow and somehow *sloping*, as if the fierce, cold wind from the sea had blown them sideways. The taxi stopped outside a house with *The Haven* painted on the lighted fanlight above the door. It was a particularly tall, thin house that seemed to lean against the much bigger house next door to it – a large, looming building with a heavy, pillared porch and dark, empty windows. 'That must be the house they used to live in,' John whispered, while Aunt Mabel paid the taxi driver. 'It looks spooky ...'

Inside *The Haven*, it was almost as cold as it was outside. The hall was narrow and high and smelt musty. There was a closed door on the left. 'That's the dining room,' Aunt Mabel said. 'Of course, we don't use it in the winter.'

They went to the end of the hall and down some narrow stairs to the basement. Here there was a big kitchen and at one end of it there was a black, menacing looking object from which came a steady whispering sound.

'Thank heavens the Beast is still alight,' Aunt Mabel said cheerfully. She smiled at their surprised faces. 'I call it the Beast,' she said. 'It won't hurt you, though.' She opened a little door in the front of the old, black boiler and a lovely shaft of warmth extended into the kitchen. They stood in front of it, thankfully warming their frozen hands. 'You look like a lot of shivering monkeys,' Aunt Mabel said. 'Come on now, move about and get warm. Which one of you is going to lay the table for me?'

The children looked at her, then at each other. Rather slowly, Mary came away from the fire and looked at the things Aunt Mabel was taking out of the dresser cupboard and putting on the deal table; a pile of mats, a bundle of knives and forks and spoons, four glasses. She tried to remember how the table always looked at home, how the knives and forks went and which side of the mat you put the glasses but both her brain and her fingers seemed numbed with cold.

'Hurry up,' Aunt Mabel said. 'Good heavens child, haven't you laid a table before?'

Mary shook her head, feeling shy and ashamed. She said, 'Jason always lays the table at home,' and her eyes filled with tears.

Aunt Mabel clicked her tongue against her teeth. 'I forgot you'd been waited on hand and foot. Well, *I* haven't the time for that. Or the inclination, I may as well tell you. So you'd better start learning to do a few things for yourself.'

In spite of her sharp voice, she explained how to lay a table patiently and clearly and Mary quite enjoyed doing it. She decided that it would be fun to learn how to do things in a house – perhaps she could make beds and clean windows and so on. At the back of her mind was the idea that in this terrible, cold climate it might be just as well to make yourself useful *indoors*. Perhaps John had the same idea because after they had had supper, he offered to help wash up, but after looking at the three weary little faces, Aunt Mabel said that it would be more sensible to go to bed.

They were to sleep up in the attic, as all the other rooms were furnished for the paying guests. They trooped, one by one up the narrow stairs, past what seemed like endless closed doors.

'Are all the rooms really *empty*?' John whispered, half fearfully, glancing along a long, dark passage.

'Yes.' Aunt Mabel thrust open one of the doors. 'You may as well look now,' she said. 'Then there'll be no need for you to go poking about when my back's turned.'

They peered into a dim, high-ceilinged room which had a big bed in the middle of it, shrouded in a white sheet. The light from the street lamp outside came through the window and made dark, eerie shadows in the corners. John clutched at Mary's hand and she could feel him shiver.

He said in a small voice, 'It'll be funny living in a house where the rooms are all shut up and empty, won't it?'

Mary squeezed his hand sympathetically. She didn't think the empty rooms were frightening, only rather dreary, but she knew that John was much more nervous in some ways than she was. He wasn't a coward, he was a normal, strong, healthy boy, but he often saw ghosts and other alarming, shadowy things in places where Mary very seldom saw them and Ben never saw them at all. Ben was a very practical person who was only afraid of good solid things that he knew were dangerous, like charging elephants and angry rhino.

Aunt Mabel shut the door with a bang and said, to John, 'It seems you've got more imagination than is good for you.'

The house seemed very quiet and still but as they reached the second landing they heard something – a low muttering that gradually got louder and louder until it burst into a deep, vibrating roar. The children stood stock still. The roar seemed to shake the house; then, suddenly, it stopped short in a loud snort and a sniffle.

They heard nothing more for a moment. Then, from behind them, they heard another queer sound. It was Aunt Mabel, laughing.

'That's Mr Agnew,' she said. 'He snores. He has a quite exceptional snore. In the summer he sleeps out in his shed in the garden so he won't disturb the other guests.'

'But it's only seven o'clock,' Ben said. 'Why should a grown-up man be asleep at seven o'clock?'

Aunt Mabel said crisply, 'Mr Agnew is an artist. Artists

aren't ordinary people. Mr Agnew likes to sleep at funny times – sometimes he sleeps all day. I expect he'll wake up soon and want his lunch.'

The children looked at each other. Mary said, cautiously, 'Where does Miss Pin live?'

'On the ground floor, because of her arthritis,' Aunt Mabel said. 'Not that it matters much where she is. She never leaves her room.'

The children digested this information in silence. What odd people they must be, Miss Pin who never went out, Mr Agnew who slept during the day.

Aunt Mabel seemed to know what they were thinking. 'There's no harm in people being a bit different,' she said. 'Miss Pin is *very* different, you'll find. Live and let live, that's my motto.'

The third flight of stairs seemed steeper than ever. Ben groaned. 'My legs will be worn out, climbing.'

'He's not used to stairs,' Mary explained. 'Our bungalow didn't have stairs.'

'He'll get used to them,' Aunt Mabel said. 'I daresay there'll be a lot of things you'll all have to get used to. Here we are now. This is your room.'

She switched on the light. The attic was long and low and bare-looking, with little, pointed, uncurtained windows. There was very little furniture in it, but the three beds looked neat and inviting and against one wall stood an enormous rocking horse with a saddle and stirrups, painted all over with bright, red spots.

Ben screamed with delight and climbed on to its back.

'I thought you might like it,' Aunt Mabel said. 'It's only an old thing – been up here for years.'

'But it looks *new*,' John said. 'Quite, quite new.'

'Oh – I painted it up a bit,' Aunt Mabel said. She sounded embarrassed.

Ben hurled himself off the horse and leapt at her, twining his small stout legs round her, hanging round her neck. 'Oh you are *kind*,' he said.

Aunt Mabel let him kiss her, but she didn't look as if she enjoyed it much. Then she untangled his legs and arms and set him firmly down on the floor. Ben said, as if something had just struck him, 'Have you got any children, Aunt Mabel?'

Aunt Mabel looked at him. There was a very odd expression on her face. 'No,' she said. Then the blood came up into her cheeks and she looked very red and cross. 'Get straight into bed,' she said. 'No romping about. You can turn out your own light. I've got quite enough to do without traipsing up and down stairs. Good night.'

When she had gone they undressed in silence. Ben and Mary got into bed and John pulled a chair up to one of the pointed windows. He wrestled with the rusty catch and pushed it open. The cold wind rushed in like icy breath, and they could hear the roaring, slithering sound of the sea crashing down on a pebble beach.

'This bed's horrible,' Ben said. 'All lumps. And it's *cold*. Shut the window, John.'

'Not for a minute. I like it.'

Mary thought that this was the first night of her life that she had gone to bed without someone kissing her good night. Even Mrs Epsom had touched her cheek with her lips when she tucked her up. She lay, thinking about this, and listening to the sea. It sounded very wild and lonely and strange; there was so much of it, she thought, between England and Africa. And Dad was thousands and thousands of miles away, on the other side.

Her eyelids felt very heavy and she closed them. As she drifted into sleep, she could hear the sea and John's voice, droning on and on, half talking to her, half talking to himself.

'If I lean out, I can see the garden. And a high wall and the big garden next door. I should think it's all overgrown and tangly. The house next door juts out much more than this house – it's like a huge dark shoulder that you can't see past. It's funny to think of such a big house being shut up for years and years except for just a little bit, in the summer. I wonder what it's like inside? All dusty and dark, I should think, with lots of rooms that no one's been into for years. On the other side of this wall there's an attic full of things no one ever sees. It would be a lovely place to hide and have a secret. Mary – that's what we'll call it. *Mary*.'

But Mary was asleep. So was Ben – fast asleep on his front with his bottom sticking up in the air. John looked at them both and then turned back to the window. He whispered to himself, 'I shall call it the House of Secrets.'

2. Mr Agnew, Miss Pin and the Face at the Window

John was awake before the others the next morning. The bare attic was flooded with clear sunlight and when he climbed up on to the rickety chair to look out of the window, he saw a pale blue sky with little clouds floating high up in it, like puffs of smoke. At the end of the garden was a line of houses with blue slate roofs and, behind them, a darker blue line where the sky met the sea. Everywhere, gulls were diving and screaming, making a tremendous noise that almost drowned the rhythmic sucking sound of the sea on the beach.

The garden immediately below the window was long and bare and narrow; at the end of it, there was a wooden shed. The garden of the big house on the other side of the high brick wall, was much larger and looked dense and overgrown with a thick shrubbery of dark, speckly evergreens.

John jumped off the chair. 'Wake up,' he said, 'Mary, *wake up*. Come and look at the sea.'

Mary yawned sleepily and rolled over in bed.

Ben sat up and sneezed so hard that his bed rattled.

Mary opened her eyes. 'You've caught a cold,' she said accusingly.

'I habend.' Ben glared at her before he sneezed again. He said in a hoarse voice, 'I habend gotta code.'

Aunt Mabel thought differently.

'You'll stay indoors this morning,' she said, after Ben had sneezed his way through breakfast. (Ben had never had a cold before and he had no idea how to be polite about it. When he wanted to sneeze, he just sneezed: it was like sitting at a table with an erupting volcano.) 'John and Mary can go out,' Aunt Mabel went on. 'But you must stay with me.'

'I don't want to,' Ben said. 'I want to go out. It'll make me worse to stay in a stuffy old house.'

'You'll do as you're told,' Aunt Mabel said.

She spoke rather sharply. She thought Ben was likely to be more difficult to control than John and Mary. She was probably right. Ben wasn't really spoiled or even particularly naughty, but he was a tough, determined little boy who had been simply used to having his own way. Up to now, there had been no real reason why he shouldn't have it. In Africa, there had been no need for a lot of tiresome rules; since his parents had known Ben was sensible enough to keep out of danger, they had let him go more or less where he liked and do what he liked. The first person who had tried to hedge him in was Mrs Epsom with her endless, boring, 'Don't do this . . . don't do that.' It seemed to Ben, suddenly, that Aunt Mabel was going to be just like her, and he went dark red with anger.

'I won't,' he said. 'I *won't*. I wan' to go and look at the sea. I habend gotta code.' And he gave a simply tremendous sneeze.

Perhaps if Aunt Mabel had laughed at him, it would have been all right. But she didn't. She was too worried in case Ben would not obey her. She knew very little about children; certainly, she had no idea how to manage Ben any more than she would have known how to manage a strange wild animal suddenly dumped down in her kitchen.

She said briskly, 'Don't be so stupid. I won't have it. If you go out, you might get pneumonia and I've got enough to do without nursing a sick child. If you don't do what you're told, you'll have to go straight up to your room and stay there.'

Ben looked at Aunt Mabel and Aunt Mabel looked at Ben. If Mary hadn't been so nervous about what was going to happen, she might have noticed that they both looked rather alike for the moment, staring at each other with the same angry, determined expression in their brown eyes. Then the colour vanished from Ben's face and he looked as white as a piece of paper, with two dark holes for eyes.

'I hate you,' he said. 'I *hate* you.' And he flew at Aunt Mabel, whirling his arms like a small windmill in a gale.

She caught hold of him by the wrists. She slapped him once, on his bare, sturdy legs. Then she took him by the collar and marched him out of the room with a grim expression on her face.

Mary and John stood still, feeling shocked and unhappy. John crept to the door and listened, but there was no sound from upstairs. They waited for about five minutes, until Aunt Mabel came back into the kitchen, stalked past them without a glance and bent over to poke the Beast. She riddled violently, so many hair pins tinkling on to the floor that her bun became unfastened and her hair fell down like a curling grey snake. She slammed the boiler door and turned to face them, two red spots high up on her cheeks, hands on hips, feet firmly planted at ten to two. She was wearing a pair of flat, flappy houseshoes; Mary thought that they made her feet look rather like a pair of kippers. She said curtly, 'Ben's got to learn to do what he's told. But that's no reason why you should hang about looking like a pair of miseries. Get your coats on and go down to the sea – a bit of air will do you good.'

Mary said nervously. 'If you don't mind, Aunt Mabel, we – we'd rather not go without Ben the first time. We'd rather wait until his cold is better.'

Aunt Mabel looked at her. Then she shrugged her shoulders and said grudgingly, 'All right. I don't mind what you do as long as you clear out from under my feet.' She began to clear the table. Mary started to help her, but she said, 'I'll do this – if you want to help you can go and tell Mr Agnew his breakfast will be ready in ten minutes.'

John looked doubtfully at Mary. 'Where is Mr Agnew?'

'Shed at bottom of garden. Put your coats on. Wind's bitter.'

They went up the basement stairs and along the passage to the back door. The long, thin garden was empty and bare-looking, even when the summer came, John thought, nothing much would ever grow there. A sound of hammering came from the wooden shed and on a nail outside the open door a man's jacket was hanging. It wasn't an ordinary looking jacket – it was huge, immense, more like an overcoat. The children stared at it, amazed. John whispered, 'He must be the biggest man in the world ...'

'Ssh,' Mary said, because Mr Agnew had suddenly appeared in the doorway. He *was* big – a vast, red-haired giant with piercing blue eyes under shaggy brows and great, hairy, gingery arms emerging from a short-sleeved red shirt. 'Well,' he said. 'What is it? Who are you?' He looked and sounded very fierce.

'Please,' Mary said in a small voice, 'Please, Aunt Mabel said to tell you breakfast is almost ready.'

He looked down at her, frowning. Then his brow cleared and he laughed, a great, resounding laugh that echoed round the narrow, walled garden like thunder. The children understood why his snore was so loud – everything about Mr Agnew was larger than life. 'Why – it's the Orphanage,' he said. He clapped a big, hammy hand on each of their shoulders. 'Come in,' he said. 'Come into the workshop.'

'We're not orphans,' John said with dignity, but Mr

Agnew did not appear to hear him. He propelled them into the shed. In the centre of the wooden floor stood a great lump of some sort of stone, taller even than Mr Agnew. 'Well,' he said, 'what do you think of it? Don't be afraid – just tell me.'

The children looked at the statue in silence.

'What is it?' Mary said.

Mr Agnew gave an explosive snort. 'Can't you see? D'you mean to tell me you can't *see*?'

'I can,' John said unexpectedly.

Mr Agnew bent his bright blue gaze upon him. 'Well?' he said in a threatening voice.

'It's a fat woman,' John said. 'Kneeling.'

They didn't understand why Mr Agnew should laugh at that, but he did, longer and louder than he had laughed before. His big stomach shook like jelly, tears streamed down his cheeks, he began to gasp for breath and ended in a kind of hoot like a ship's siren, *Hoo, hoo, hoo* . . . John and Mary watched him, astonished. Finally, he wiped his eyes and said in a choking voice, 'That's good. That's rich. My Venus, my beautiful Venus – fat woman, kneeling. *Hoo, hoo* . . .' He slapped the statue affectionately with his hand. 'That's brought me down a peg. D'you know, I think that's what I shall call her.'

He stood for a moment, gazing at the statue and rasping his hand over his plump, unshaven chin. He seemed to have forgotten the children altogether.

John said, 'Your breakfast's ready, Mr Agnew.'

'What? Oh . . .' He smiled at John. 'Don't call me Mr Agnew. Call me Uncle Abe. Honorary Uncle.' He reached his jacket down from the hook and began to put it on. 'Do you like messing about with clay? There's some terracotta on that bench. See what you can do with it.'

He picked up two lumps of the red clay, big as footballs,

and tossed one to each of them. Mary looked at hers, and then at the front of her coat. 'It's very kind of you,' she said. 'But – but Aunt Mabel might be cross.' She thought of Mrs Epsom. 'If we get dirty, I mean.'

Uncle Abe drew his bristly eyebrows together. 'You're not afraid of Mabel, surely?' He looked searchingly at their downcast faces. 'Good Lord – I believe you are.' He sounded as if the idea astonished him and made him rather angry. 'You needn't be, y'know,' he said, frowning sternly. 'Your Aunt's an angel. Understand that? An Angel.' He glared at them, turned on his heel and marched towards the house.

'She's a funny sort of angel,' John said thoughtfully.

'Yes.' Mary sighed and looked up at the top floor of *The Haven*, at the tiny attic window that glinted in the sun. 'Poor Ben. He must be awfully miserable,' she said.

But Ben wasn't miserable, he was far too angry. No one had ever slapped him before or punished him in any way. He sat on the edge of his little bed, rebellion and fury burning in his heart, muttering crossly under his breath. He had sneezed so much that his head ached. When he had been angry in Africa, he had always gone off on his own, with Balthazar, until he felt better. He began to think about Balthazar and how he would probably never see him again and after a little while he began to feel comfortably sad and a lot less angry. He thought that it had been rather unkind of him to tell Aunt Mabel that he hated her. Perhaps it had made her cry. He hadn't really meant to make her cry. He thought she had probably not meant to be so cross with him and that she might easily feel unhappy about it now. He decided that he would go and find her – not to say he was sorry, because he didn't think he had done anything wrong – but so that *she* could say she was sorry to *him*.

He crept down the stairs, rather cautiously just in case she wasn't feeling as sorry as she ought to feel, just yet, and stood at the top of the basement stairs. He was just going to start down to the kitchen when he heard a deep, man's voice and then Aunt Mabel's, answering him. Ben sighed. It was no good going down to the kitchen if she wasn't alone, she would just shoo him back to his room. He decided to explore a little instead. He peered into the big, silent dining room that smelt musty and shut up and had lots of tables with chairs stuck up on top of them. There was a big, dark sideboard with lots of bottles of sauce on it and a grandfather clock in the corner that ticked with a fat, comfortable sound. Ben unscrewed the tops of some of the bottles and tasted the sauces with his tongue. Then he found a glass and a spoon in a cupboard in the sideboard and tried making a mixture to drink. He mixed and tasted and mixed and tasted until his tongue felt rather sore. So he cleaned the glass and the spoon, very carefully with his dirty handkerchief, and put them back.

Further along the passage, there was a closed door. Ben wondered if it led into another empty room; he was just about to turn the handle when he thought he heard someone talking inside. Not quite *someone*, though – it had been a thin, squeaky sound, rather like a mouse talking. He waited for a little, then, very quietly, he opened the door and went in.

He must have been wrong, he thought, because there was no one there. It was a small room, and very dark. Thick velvet curtains hung at the window, leaving only a narrow slit for the light to come through. The walls seemed to be hung with rich, dark red material that had gold thread woven into it. Above the mantelpiece there was a big picture in a heavy gilt frame, but it was so dark that Ben could not see what it was meant to be. The room was very full of chests and little tables – so full, in fact, that there was barely room to walk. In front of the fireplace there was a perfectly ordinary wooden towel horse with clothes folded over it that looked out of place, Ben thought, in this rather grand, gloomy room. Near the towel horse, Ben saw something that interested him. On a small, carved table, there was a collection of miniature china and some small, pretty figures carved in a kind of green, cloudy glass. Ben threaded his way through the furniture, being very careful not to knock anything over, and picked up a tiny cup painted with green and yellow flowers.

Behind him a voice said, 'Careful, Boy. That piece is valuable.'

He was so startled that he almost dropped the cup. He put it down gently on the table and said, severely, 'You made me jump.'

There *was* someone in the room after all, watching him with eyes that were dark and shiny as boot buttons. The clothes horse was being used as a screen, and inside the screen, in front of a tall oil stove, sat a little old woman in a brilliantly coloured shawl and a queer hat that was all feathers. Beneath the hat her tiny face peeped out; it was wrinkled all over and a pale, yellowish colour. Although she was wearing a shawl and the feather hat, her feet were bare and resting in an enamel bath steaming with hot water. She held a kettle in her lap; another sizzled on the top of the oil stove.

'Who are you?' Ben said, rather rudely.

The old woman's eyes snapped. 'I think that is a question I should ask *you*.'

'I'm Ben Mallory,' Ben said.

She bowed her head in a queenly way so that all the feathers dipped and waved.

'I am Muriel Pin. Delighted to make your acquaintance.'

She was wearing long, black gloves. Very slowly, she

took the right one off. Her fingers were thin and frail looking and covered with rings that flashed as she held out her hand. Ben took it and they shook hands gravely.

'Are you cold?' Ben said.

'Yes, I am, Mr Mallory. How very intelligent of you to observe – people seldom do. Mrs Haggard, now, thinks I am simply eccentric.' Her voice sank to a thread of a whisper. 'I believe she thinks I am a little *mad*. Mad Muriel, she calls me behind my back – she thinks I don't know it. Servants have no respect nowadays.'

'I'm cold too,' Ben said. He thought the hot bath and the kettles were a very sensible way of keeping warm. 'I've been cold ever since I came to England.'

Miss Pin placed her ungloved hand against the side of the kettle on her lap. 'Getting cool,' she said. She exchanged it for the kettle on the oil stove, poured more hot water into the bath and then held the empty kettle towards Ben. 'Would you mind filling this up for me, Mr Mallory. Over in the corner – *there*.' She pointed with a scrawny finger.

In the corner there was a brown velvet curtain that rattled back on brass rings and revealed a washbasin. Ben filled the kettle carefully – it was rather a tricky business – and took it back.

'Put it down here,' the old lady commanded. 'No, no, stupid boy ... can't you see?' She bent sideways and picked up something from the floor. 'This is Sir Lancelot,' she said. She showed him a small tortoise with a green ribbon tied round his shell. She spoke to it in the thin, squeaky voice Ben had heard through the door. 'Sir Lancelot – meet Mr Benjamin Mallory.' The tortoise slid out his scaly old head and blinked black eyes at Ben. 'He suffers with the cold, as I do. Sometimes I give him baths in warm olive oil. You may stroke his chin, if you care to.'

Gently, Ben stroked the dry old chin. He said, 'Do tortoises like that? I wish I had a pet. In Africa, I had a chameleon.' He thought perhaps Miss Pin would like to hear about Balthazar, so he sat down on a red leather stool beside the enamel bath, and told her about him. She seemed very interested.

'Tell me about Africa,' she said, her boot-button eyes glistening. 'It must be a very wild, strange place. I have always wished to travel but my Dear Papa never allowed it, though he, of course, spent much of his life in India. Until his Enemies hounded him out, of course. When that happened, we fled to Henstable.' She gave a little sigh. 'We came here when I was a child of ten and I have never left it since.'

'How old are you?' Ben asked.

'Eighty-two.'

Ben drew a deep breath. He looked at her face and her shawl and her feathered hat and thought he had never seen anyone so odd-looking, or so old. 'Who are the Enemies?' he said.

'Hush.' Miss Pin leaned forward in her chair, hunching herself up until she looked like a crooked old witch. 'Don't speak so loud. They are all around us – watching and listening. You need not be afraid, though. We are quite safe, here in this house. That is why Dear Papa named it *The Haven*. Even should They force their way in, there are places to hide. Places where They would never find us. You're *not* afraid, are you?'

'Of course not,' Ben said boldly, though her secretive, whispering voice sent delicious shivers running up and down his spine. 'If They came in, though – the Enemies, I mean, where would you hide?'

She said slowly, 'I don't know that I should tell you. Can you keep a secret?' She looked at him thoughtfully. 'I believe you can. You're a sensible boy, aren't you?'

Ben nodded, hugging his knees. He thought she was the most interesting grown-up he had met for a long time.

She took the kettle off the oil stove, tested the temperature, and placed it on her lap. 'When we came here,' she said, 'I thought this a very old house. So poky – so different from our grand house in London. I was a very lonely child – Dear Papa would not allow me to mix with other children in case I should meet an Enemy, you see. I had everything a child could want, we were very rich, you see, because of all the treasure Papa had brought home from India, but for most of the time I was very dull. Then, one afternoon when Cook was out, I discovered the secret passage. I was exploring the cellar ...'

'What is a cellar?' Ben said.

In his excitement, he spoke much too loudly. Aunt Mabel who was outside in the passage, heard him and thrust open the door. 'Ben, you naughty boy,' she said in an exasperated voice. 'I thought I told you to stay in your room?' She seized Ben's arm and jerked him crossly up from his stool. 'Do as I tell you another time. I'm sorry he's bothered you, Miss Pin.'

Miss Pin was sitting very upright in her chair. In spite of her funny hat and her bare feet and the kettle in her lap, Ben thought she looked grand and imperious, rather like a queen. She spoke like a queen, too.

'You are exceeding your duties, Mrs Haggard. Mr Mallory is a friend of mine. I am pleased to have him visit me.'

'Oh. Oh well, if you say so ...' Aunt Mabel sounded rather flustered. 'But you'll tire yourself – you know the doctor said you weren't to tire yourself.' In spite of her grumpy voice, Ben saw that she was very gentle as she plumped up the cushions behind the old lady's back and settled her more comfortably against them.

'It tires me far more to be lonely all day,' Muriel Pin said.

She looked at Ben. 'You'll come again, won't you?' She sounded quavery and humble, suddenly, not queenly at all.

'Yes, I'll come back,' Ben said.

'I'd like to give you a present,' the old lady said. 'Come here.'

Ben stood beside her, while she selected a tiny horse from the little table beside her. 'Look after him,' she said. 'Papa brought him back from India.'

The horse felt cool in his hand. 'Thank you,' Ben said, 'He's *lovely*. I'll take care of him for *ever*.'

'Come along Ben, do,' Aunt Mabel said, from the door.

When they were outside in the passage, she marched him along it until they were safely out of earshot. Then she took his shoulder and turned him to face her. She said sternly, 'Listen to me, Ben. You're not to bother Miss Pin, whatever she says. She's old and sick. Let me see what she gave you.'

Rather reluctantly, Ben showed her the little, pale green horse.

Aunt Mabel sighed. 'Well, I suppose she can spare that, she's got enough old junk. It'll be one thing less for me to dust. But you're not to take anything else. Or ask for anything. Do you understand that? She's a poor old woman and she can't afford to give greedy little boys presents.'

Ben was furiously angry. 'I wouldn't ask for presents. And anyway, she's *not* poor. She's rich. She told me.' He was so cross that he went red, right to the tips of his ears.

Aunt Mabel looked at him. Then she shrugged her shoulders. She said, half to herself, 'I suppose it's harmless enough.' She glanced at her watch. 'Your cold sounds better to me. It won't hurt you to run along into the garden with the others.'

When Ben ran into the garden, he was bursting to tell Mary and John about Miss Pin and to show them his little horse. But they were far too preoccupied to listen to him. They were standing halfway down the garden, staring up at the big, neglected old house on the other side of the high brick wall. The sun had moved round in the sky and the windows were all in shadow. They looked very blank and empty.

'But I *did* see it,' John was saying in an excited voice. 'I did, I *did*.'

'What did you see?' Ben panted up to them, the little horse clasped tightly in his hand.

Mary laughed. 'John *thinks* he saw someone in the house next door but he couldn't have, because the house is empty. Aunt Mabel said so. So he's just being silly.'

'I'm *not*.' John went red. He hated it when Mary laughed at him. He was breathing rather fast and his hands were clenched in front of him. 'I'm sure I saw a face – a face at the window.'

3. The Secret Passage

The house next door belonged to a man called Mr Reynolds. He was an art collector, Aunt Mabel told John, and the house was full of paintings and other treasures he had brought from all over the world.

'He's got a big house in London as well,' Aunt Mabel said, '*and* a castle somewhere in France. It's my belief that he bought my house chiefly to have somewhere else to hang all his pictures – though what pleasure he gets out of them, I can't think. He hasn't been down here for at least two years.'

It seemed queer to John that someone should buy a lot of pictures and hang them up in a house he never visited. It made the house next door seem more mysterious than ever. John wished he could get inside it to find out what it was like but he didn't say so to Mary. He was afraid she would laugh at him, as she had laughed when he told her he had seen the face at the window. He had only seen it for a moment, a dim, pale blur at one of the top floor windows, and after a little while he began to think he must have imagined it. No one could possibly get inside the house; it seemed so very empty and shut up and the garden walls were so high. John thought it was sad that a house should be so silent and unwanted and wondered if it would feel different from other houses that were used and lived in.

It was partly because he was an imaginative boy that he thought so much about the house, and partly because he had very little else to do. Mary was busy helping Aunt Mabel – she made the beds and went shopping and washed up the dishes – and Ben spent as much time as he could with Miss

Pin. Neither Mary nor John knew what they talked about, shut up in that dark, stuffy room, but they could hear their voices droning on and on behind the closed door, like bees on a summer day.

'What do you talk about all the time?' John asked Ben.

'Oh – just things,' Ben said mysteriously. 'About olden times when she was a girl. It's like a story. She tells lovely stories.'

Aunt Mabel seemed to be glad that Ben liked Miss Pin. She let him carry in her trays at meal-times and fill up her kettles and answer the little brass cow bell that she rang whenever she wanted anything. 'It saves my legs,' Aunt Mabel said.

One Saturday morning, when the children had been in Henstable for two months, Aunt Mabel was busier than ever. A man had telephoned from London the night before to ask for a room for the weekend; he had said that if he liked *The Haven*, he might stay longer. Aunt Mabel said it was a stroke of luck to get someone at this time of the year; she asked Mary to help her clean out one of the guest rooms and make the bed and she sent John to buy a chicken from the fishmonger.

The visitor arrived just before lunchtime. Peeping over the banisters, the children saw a small, pale man with a high, bald forehead and two pointed, yellow teeth that stuck out in front of his mouth. He didn't come upstairs to see the room that Mary had helped Aunt Mabel get ready for him, but went straight into the dining room, leaving his suitcase standing in the hall. Aunt Mabel showed him to a table, then came out again and whispered up to the children, 'You'll have to wait for your lunch.'

The children waited, crouching together on the stairs. They saw Aunt Mabel come up from the basement carrying the visitor's lunch on a tray. There was a chicken, brown and still spitting from the oven and separate little dishes of peas, carrots and potatoes, all glistening with butter. Ben's mouth watered. 'Do you think he'll eat it all? Every bit?' he said wistfully.

Aunt Mabel came out of the dining room with an empty tray and disappeared down to the kitchen. When she reappeared, ten minutes later, she was carrying the pudding – crusty apple pie with a jug of wrinkled, yellow cream. She smiled cheerfully at the children before she went into the dining room but when she came out again she didn't look cheerful at all. Her face was stiff and anxious. On the tray was the lovely, crisp chicken. It was barely touched.

Ben whispered, 'Golly – did you see? There'll be lots left for us!' He smacked his lips with a juicy noise and rubbed his stomach.

'Don't be silly,' Mary said sharply. 'If he hasn't eaten the chicken – it means he doesn't like it. And if he doesn't like the food, he won't stay.'

John said, 'Perhaps he doesn't like first courses. Perhaps he only likes pudding. And it's a lovely apple pie.'

They watched anxiously while Aunt Mabel took in the coffee and brought out the remains of the pudding. He had hardly eaten anything – just the smallest hole had been made in the side of the sugar-dusted crust. Aunt Mabel didn't look up at the children. She stumped straight down to the kitchen.

'Perhaps he wasn't hungry Or perhaps he's a vegetarian,' John suggested hopefully.

'Vegetarians eat apple pie,' Mary said.

They were silent for a minute. Then Ben said, 'He'll have to pay for it anyway, won't he?'

'I don't know.' There was a little frown on Mary's forehead. She was thinking of how hard Aunt Mabel had worked to make the house look nice and cook a good lunch.

And of how much the chicken and the cream had cost. Everything cost a lot – even gas, for cooking. The Gas Bill had arrived at breakfast time and Aunt Mabel had sighed when she saw it.

Then the visitor came out into the hall. He was wiping his mouth with his handkerchief and looking round him in a lost sort of way.

John whispered, 'Perhaps he wants to go to the bathroom.'

Mary stood up. She wasn't quite sure what she was going to say but she knew she was going to say something and it made her feel shaky and queer. She went a little way down the stairs and said in a loud voice, 'Do you want anything?' The man looked up, startled, and she went on quickly, 'I'm afraid you didn't eat much of your nice lunch. I hope it was because you just weren't hungry, not because you didn't like it.'

The man didn't answer. He simply stared at Mary with his pale eyes. Although he had eaten so little, he hadn't been very tidy about it: there were food stains on his waistcoat and on his tie. Mary felt dreadfully nervous but she took a deep breath and went on, 'We hope you'll like our boarding-house and stay here for a long time because Aunt Mabel needs lots of money to pay the Gas Bill and things like that.'

'Good heavens,' the visitor said. 'Good heavens.' He looked quite astonished and rather angry. He glared at Aunt Mabel who had come into the hall while Mary had been talking. She gave him a stiff, apologetic smile, marched to the foot of the stairs and said in an icy voice, 'Mary – all of you – go down to the kitchen this minute.'

They went, in silence. Aunt Mabel followed them. When she had closed the kitchen door she said, 'Mary, you are a naughty, impertinent girl. Please remember in future that you are not to speak to my guests or bother them in any way

This gentleman is an important man in the City – he has come down here to have a rest, not to be badgered by rude children.' She was very white and shaking.

Ben said, 'He doesn't look like an important man. He looks just like a *rabbit*.' And he giggled suddenly, his hand across his mouth.

'He looks like your bread and butter,' Aunt Mabel said. 'Don't you forget it.' And she went out and shut the door.

No one spoke for a minute. Mary was staring hard at the floor, the blood burning in her cheeks.

Then Ben said, 'What did she mean? Why does he look like our bread and butter?'

John looked at Mary and said slowly, 'I think she means what she said in the train – that she gets all her money from visitors who come and stay here. And unless people come and stay and pay her for it, she can't buy food for *us*.'

Ben shrugged his shoulders. 'I don't like bread and butter,' he said. 'I like bread and butter and *jam*.'

In the afternoon, Aunt Mabel sent them down to the sea and told them to stay out of the visitor's way until tea time.

It was very cold. Although it was March, none of the daffodils in the gardens had opened and even the buds looked pinched and cold as if the sharp winds had frozen them. As for the sea – the children thought they had never seen anything so grey and wild, not at all like the sea at Mombasa in Kenya where you could swim all day and see marvellous fish and rocks if you dived under the clear, blue water.

Since they came to England, they had spent a great deal of time by this chilly sea because Aunt Mabel had decided they were not to go to school until the Summer Term. They had all caught coughs and colds and when she took them to the doctor, he said, 'No school for a bit. They're perfectly healthy, but they've lived in Africa for so long that they haven't any resistance to English germs. Let them run about and get used to the climate.'

They *had* to run about most of the time, to keep warm. It was so cold that Mary and John had chilblains on their fingers and toes that itched and burned whenever they were indoors by the fire. Aunt Mabel put ointment on the chilblains and gave them cough mixture for their chests. She was kind to them in that sort of way – a brisk, rather impersonal way like a nurse or a schoolteacher. But she never once kissed them good night or asked if they were happy. Mary sometimes thought that if she hadn't got John and Ben, she might have felt very sad and lonely indeed.

'She's not cross, exactly,' she said to John, 'I think it's just that she doesn't like us much.'

They were sitting on the beach in the shelter of a slimy, green breakwater, throwing stones into an old tin can that John had stuck up on a pole. Ben was looking for cockles in a patch of shiny mud left by the outgoing tide. He was crouching on his haunches, watching for the tell-tale wriggle in the mud and then burrowing with his fingers to find the tiny, pink-shelled creatures that Uncle Abe liked to eat for tea.

'She's not used to liking people,' John said. 'I mean – she's never had a family to practise on, has she? And I think she's worried because it costs so much to feed us and mend our shoes and that sort of thing.'

'Why doesn't Dad send her some money, then?'

John frowned. 'Perhaps he hasn't got any. After all, the house was swept away and everything. Or perhaps he hasn't thought about it. You know how vague he is – Mother always paid the bills, didn't she?' He went rather pink, suddenly, and threw a stone very hard at the tin.

'Well, what about Uncle Abe and Miss Pin? I mean – if

the rabbity man looked like our bread-and-butter why don't they?'

'I don't think they pay anything,' John said surprisingly. 'You remember Uncle Abe said she was an angel? Well, it couldn't be because she's so sweet and kind, could it? So I think he said it because she lets him stay *free*.'

'Did he tell you that?' Mary said.

'No. I guessed because he never sells any of his statues and all his clothes are so awful. But he *did* tell me about Miss Pin. He was showing me how to model a head in his workshop yesterday and he said, where was Ben, and *I* said he was helping Aunt Mabel clean Miss Pin's room – you know she lets him dust her little animals and things – and Uncle Abe said it was a blessing Ben got on so well with the old lady because it took some of the weight off Aunt Mabel's shoulders. I asked him if Miss Pin had always lived here and he said yes, she's been a lodger at *The Haven* for as long as anyone could remember. Long before Aunt Mabel bought it. Uncle Abe said Miss Pin had a niece who used to pay her bills, but when Aunt Mabel took over the boarding-house, the niece came down to see her and said she couldn't afford to pay any longer and Miss Pin would have to go into a Home. But Aunt Mabel wouldn't hear of it; she said as long as she had her health and strength the poor old soul could stay with her, and welcome.'

'I think that was very nice of Aunt Mabel,' Mary said slowly.

'Uncle Abe said she has a heart of gold. But as soon as he'd said it, he gave one of his funny laughs and said he must admit it didn't *show*. Then he stopped laughing and said I'd learn when I got older that people weren't always what they seemed to be. He said Aunt Mabel was really a very loving sort of person but she hadn't had anyone to love for so long that she'd got out of the habit.'

Mary said, 'I suppose she must have been awfully sad when her husband was drowned. I remember Dad said he was quite young and they hadn't been married long.' Mary felt tears prickling behind her eyes. She turned her head away so that John shouldn't see and said, 'There's one thing I don't understand, though. Ben says Miss Pin is *rich*.'

'She's batty,' John said scornfully.

Ben heard him say that. He had just come up with his pail full of cockles. 'She's not,' he said angrily. 'She's nice. And she knows a lot of things you don't know. She's told me some of them. She knows something *you* don't know about the house.'

'What?'

'Shan't tell you.' Ben glared at John. He had got thinner since they had come to Henstable and his eyes looked bigger and darker than they used to look. He stamped his foot and said, '*She* wouldn't tell you either. You're too mean and horrible.'

'*You* tell me, then,' John said. He got up and advanced on Ben who jumped over the breakwater and stuck out his tongue. John scrambled after him and grabbed hold of his arm. 'Come on,' he said, giving Ben a little shake, 'tell me.'

'I won't. It's a secret,' Ben said. He shook himself free and faced his brother, his dark eyes blazing.

'Stop it, both of you,' Mary said. She felt suddenly that she couldn't bear it if they quarrelled. She said coaxingly 'Let's go home – we've got to cook the cockles and it must be nearly time for tea.'

But tea wasn't ready. As they walked towards *The Haven*, they saw that a taxi had stopped outside and that the rabbity man was getting into it. Aunt Mabel was standing on the step, watching him go.

'Is he leaving?' Mary asked as they came up to her.

Aunt Mabel didn't seem to hear, she just turned on her heel and went indoors. It wasn't until they were all downstairs in the kitchen that she said, 'Yes, he's gone. Mary, lay the table, will you?'

She put the kettle on and lit the grill to make toast for tea. Her expression was so stiff and forbidding that none of the children dared say anything. When tea was ready, they sat down at the table with downcast eyes. None of them felt in the least hungry.

After about five minutes, Mary said nervously, 'Aunt Mabel – did the man go away because of what I said?'

Aunt Mabel glanced at her briefly. 'No – no, of course not. He left because his bedroom was too cold.' She gave a short laugh. 'As if a grown man would bother about what a little girl said!'

Mary felt a little better, but not much. It was kind of Aunt Mabel to say it wasn't her fault, but she had spoken in such a cold, angry way that she still felt very miserable. She sat, staring at her plate and so did John and Ben.

Looking at their faces, Aunt Mabel thought they were sulking. It didn't occur to her that they were unhappy because they thought she was dreadfully cross with them. She didn't even know she had sounded cross. She had had such a lonely, worrying life – it was even more worrying now she had three children to look after – that she had grown rather prickly and sharp-voiced without realizing it. She was a stiff, rather shy sort of person and although she would have liked to be kinder and more loving to the children, she did not really know how to begin. As a result, her brisk, unaffectionate ways froze up even Mary's kind heart and, as she sat, eating her toast, she began to think that it was all very well for Uncle Abe to say Aunt Mabel was nice and loving *underneath*. But it didn't make her any easier to live with.

*

After tea, Aunt Mabel went down to the shops to get fresh fish for Miss Pin's supper. The only kind of fish Miss Pin liked was plaice, boned and steamed in butter. As soon as she was gone, Ben said in an excited voice, 'I've got an idea.' He was very pink and his eyes shone. 'It's an idea how to make money.'

Mary and John looked at each other. They remembered that it had been Ben who had asked Aunt Mabel if she was really poor, when they were in the train coming to Henstable. He had never mentioned it since, but that was like Ben. If he had a problem he didn't talk about it, but turned it over and over in his mind until he had an answer to it. He said now, 'We can collect cockles. I saw some men on the beach collecting cockles and they said they sold them to the fish shop. *We* could do that, then Aunt Mabel would have enough money to buy lots of bread-and-butter.'

John said, 'But you can't collect enough cockles in a pail. Not enough to *sell*.'

'We want a sack, like the men had. There are lots of sacks in the cellar.'

Ben ran to a door at the far end of the kitchen, opened it, and disappeared. Mary and John followed. They had never been in the cellar and they peered cautiously down the flight of wooden stairs that led down into darkness. Ben's voice floated up to them. 'Put the light on. The switch is just inside the door.'

John switched on the light and went down the stairs. The cellar was a low, rambling, pleasant place that smelt of dry wood and dust. There was a pile of coke for the Beast in one corner, a stack of wood in another and a bench against one wall with a saw and some nails on it. Under the bench, John found a pile of sacks; he and Mary began shaking them out and choosing the two best ones.

Meanwhile, Ben roamed round the cellar. Set in the brick

wall at one end, were two arched little doors – very low, as if they had been made for dwarfs or children. Ben opened one of the doors and found a cubby hole with an earth floor and a wooden ceiling; a tiny room that would have made a splendid hide-away if it had not been full of packing cases and empty lemonade bottles. He wondered if there was another room behind the other door but when he tried to open it, it seemed to be locked or stuck.

He called out to John and Mary, 'Come and help. I think it's locked.'

'There are some keys here,' Mary said. There was a big bunch of keys hanging on a nail above the bench. She took them down and went over to the little door. John tried several keys before he found a small one that exactly fitted the lock. It was rusty and stiff; it took two hands and all his strength to turn the key, but it *did* turn and the door swung creakily open.

There was a small room behind this door, just as there was behind the other one. At first, the only difference seemed to be that this room was empty and when the children peered in, the air inside felt colder than the air in the cellar. Then they saw that high up in the wall at the back was a small, square, dark hole. A chill little wind blew out of it and a queer smell – a mixture of earth and mice and shut-upness.

'What *is* it?' Mary whispered.

No one answered for a minute. Then Ben said in a low, awestruck voice, 'It's the Secret Passage.' There was a bright, mysterious look in his eyes. He said, very fast, 'I couldn't tell you about it because Miss Pin asked me not to. But now you've found it for yourselves, it's all right, isn't it?'

He looked anxiously at Mary who took his hard little hand and said, 'Of course it's all right. But a passage must go somewhere. Does Miss Pin know where it goes?'

Ben shook his head. 'She just said it was a place to hide. But we could go and *see*, couldn't we?'

Mary said, 'I've got a torch. It was hanging up with the keys.' She looked at John. 'You go first . . .'

John drew a deep breath. It was stupid to be scared, he told himself. He was eleven, nearly twelve – nearly grown-up.

Ben said eagerly, 'I'll go. I'd like to go.' The menacing, dark hole didn't worry him at all. What could be there, after all, except a mouse or two?

John said quickly, 'No. It may be dangerous. I'm the eldest. I'll go.'

As he pulled himself up to the hole, the torch in his hand, he grinned to himself in spite of feeling so sick and clammy. If he wasn't so frightened he would be quite ready to let Ben go ahead – it would be more sensible, really. Ben was smaller and less likely to get stuck.

The hole led to a tunnel which was just high enough for John to crawl through, knees scraping on rubble. It was very short; after about two yards it opened into a much bigger place, high enough for John to kneel up. He swept the torch round and saw brick walls and rafters above his head.

'We're under the house,' Mary said, wriggling beside him. 'Oh blow – I've torn my dress. It must be the foundations of the house.'

'What a swizz,' John said in a cheerful, grumbling tone, secretly rather relieved that this was all there was – just this dry, clean place with the floors of the house above.

But it wasn't all. 'Look,' Ben squeaked. 'Give me the torch . . .'

At one side there was another hole, just above the level of the ground. This time there was no doubt about who was to go first. Ben snatched the torch from John and crawled in. His muffled voice came back to them. 'Come on – it goes on an awfully long way.'

This tunnel was very low and it was more difficult for Mary and John to get through it than for Ben. They had to squirm along on their stomachs, using their elbows and knees, and it was rather alarming because Ben was so far ahead that they couldn't see the light from the torch. Mary was so close behind John that his feet kicked dust and earth back into her face. At one place the tunnel seemed to be almost blocked by a mess of brick and rubble as if someone had tried to wall it up at some time. John called, 'Ben ...' and Ben's voice sounded hollow and strange. 'Come on ... come on, it's not far now.'

Quite suddenly, the tunnel ended. It just stopped, high up in a wall. Ben was shining the torch and John and Mary crawled out, head first, and pitched on to a pile of wood shavings. 'Just as well *that* was there,' John said, sitting up. 'Or we'd have banged our heads horribly hard. Give me the torch, Ben.'

They were in quite a big room, very dry, with a brick floor. It opened into another room with a series of cubby holes along one side, stacked with wine bottles lying on their sides. At the far end was a flight of wooden steps and a closed door at the top. John shone the torch up the steps. He caught his breath.

'Mary,' he shouted, 'Mary – do you know where we are? We're in the cellar of the house next door. We're in the House of Secrets.'

He ran up the stairs and tugged at the handle of the door, quite forgetting to be frightened in the excitement of being in the very place he had so longed to see.

But the cellar door was locked.

4. The House of Secrets

'Perhaps one of those old keys will fit,' John panted as they wriggled back through the tunnel. He was not at all frightened now, he was much too excited. He had been in the cellar of the House of Secrets. He only had to find a key – just one key – and he would be in the house itself!

Mary had left the bunch of keys on the bench in their own cellar, but when she scrambled out of the cubby hole and went to fetch them, the keys were gone. 'I'm sure I left them here,' she said in a loud, surprised voice.

'Be quiet – oh be *quiet*,' John hissed behind her. He was looking up at the cellar door, his eyes wide with alarm. It stood ajar and a familiar, rattling noise came from the kitchen. 'It's Aunt Mabel, stoking the Beast,' he said.

Mary whispered, 'She must have moved the keys. Yes – there they are, back on the nail.'

She and John looked at each other in horror. They were filthy; their clothes were black and their hair and eyebrows were whitish-grey with dust.

'We're awfully dirty. She'll be hopping mad,' Ben said cheerfully.

'She'll find out about the passage,' John said. This thought made his heart thump very fast. If Aunt Mabel knew where they had been she would almost certainly stop them going through the tunnel again and he would never see the house next door – never, ***never***. He clenched his fists and muttered, 'I couldn't bear it, I couldn't.' He looked frantically at Mary. 'What can we say? She must have been down here to get the coke for the Beast – she'll know we weren't just playing in the cellar.'

Mary drew a deep breath. 'Just don't say anything,' she said. 'Or you either, Ben. Just leave it to me.'

Her back was very straight and her head held very high as she marched up the cellar steps and into the kitchen. John and Ben followed her; John felt very scared, but Ben hummed a jaunty little tune under his breath. Aunt Mabel looked at them, her mouth open. 'Whatever . . .' she began.

Mary gabbled very fast, 'I'm sorry we got so dirty, Aunt Mabel. But we've been hiding in the cellar – in the cubby hole.' It was almost true, she thought, they *had* been hiding in the cubby hole, but all the same the colour came and went in her cheeks and she stared guiltily at the floor.

'So that's where you were,' Aunt Mabel said. 'I wondered what you'd been doing with those old keys.'

John said quickly, 'Do you mind us playing with them, Aunt Mabel?'

Aunt Mabel shrugged her shoulders. 'They're no use to me. Just a bunch of old keys I've had for years. As a matter of fact, I think I brought most of them from the house next door – they won't fit many of the locks here.'

John gave a little gasp, then a slow smile appeared on his face. It really was possible, then, that one of the keys would fit that cellar door. This made him feel so excited and happy that he stood, grinning to himself and looking rather foolish. Aunt Mabel gave him a curious look. Then she glanced at Mary and Ben and her lips twitched very slightly. 'You look as if you'd been climbing chimneys,' she said. 'It's a good thing you had some old clothes on.'

Her tone was quite uncomplaining and Mary suddenly realised that Aunt Mabel was not in the least like Mrs Epsom; she never made a fuss when they got dirty or tore their clothes. Then she saw a flimsy blue envelope on the table and everything else went out of her mind. 'Is that from Daddy?' she cried.

'No,' Aunt Mabel said. 'It's from Mrs Epsom. Your father has gone off on leave – Mrs Epsom says he's on safari in the Northern Frontier District.' She picked the letter up and put it in her apron pocket. 'I expect he'll send you a postcard.'

Ben laughed. 'He won't be able to buy postcards *there*,' he said scornfully.

'Won't he? I don't know much about Africa.' Aunt Mabel looked at the children, frowning a little as if something was worrying her. Then she said sharply, 'Run along and have a good, hot bath. Use plenty of soap. You look as if you could do with it.'

When they had gone, she sat down, took the letter out of her pocket and read it. When Uncle Abe came in for his supper a little later, she was still sitting there, staring thoughtfully and somehow sadly in front of her, the letter still in her hand.

'Anything wrong?' he asked, surprised. Aunt Mabel didn't often sit like this, doing nothing.

Aunt Mabel glanced at him. 'You'd better read this,' she said shortly.

Uncle Abe took the letter and read it. Then he folded it carefully and handed it back to her. 'Poor little beggars,' he said softly. 'Do they miss their father very much?'

'I think so,' Aunt Mabel said. 'They don't talk about him – but Mary runs to the letter box every morning. I hear her feet scampering down the passage and then coming back, very slowly. He hasn't written to them, not once. It looks as if he has quite forgotten about them. You saw what Mrs Epsom said? He seemed half out of his mind with grief . . .'

Uncle Abe blew his nose very loudly. He said, 'He must have loved their mother very much.'

'He'd have fetched her the moon out of the sky, if he could,' Aunt Mabel said in a dry voice. She drummed her fingers on the arm of her chair in the way she often did when she was thinking very hard about something. 'He wasn't in a fit state to go off into the wilds on his own. Suppose something happens to him? What will happen to the children then?'

'I daresay he'll turn up safe and sound,' Uncle Abe said slowly.

Aunt Mabel sighed. 'I hope so. They're my sister's children and I shall do my best to do my duty by them. But it won't be easy. They expect such a lot – their parents adored them, spoiled them, to my mind.'

'They don't seem spoiled to me. What do you mean?' Uncle Abe said.

Aunt Mabel shrugged her shoulders impatiently. 'Oh – they just seem to expect everyone to love them. I haven't got time to fuss over children. I can just about afford to feed them as long as they're not particular but I can't afford to give them a lot of clothes and toys. I can't afford to give them anything ...'

Uncle Abe was looking at her with an odd expression on his face. He said suddenly, 'You can give them a home. That's the most important thing. *I* know that – after all, you've given me one. Oh – I know I'm supposed to be a lodger, but when did I last pay my rent? Tell me that?' He threw out his chest and thumped it with his big fist.

'Oh – don't ask silly questions,' Aunt Mabel said. She got up from her chair and started to lay the table for supper, putting down the knives and forks with a lot of unnecessary noise.

Uncle Abe said, 'It's not a silly question. I owe you a lot of money – money that you need now, for the children.'

Aunt Mabel took no notice. Her cheeks were rather red and her eyes very bright.

Uncle Abe cleared his throat and said loudly, 'As a matter of fact, I may be able to pay you back sooner than you expect. I've got an interview tomorrow, with a man who runs a big Art Gallery in London. He wrote and said he'd like to see some of my stuff.'

Aunt Mabel smiled. She didn't often smile, but when she did it was usually at Uncle Abe who reminded her of her young husband who had been drowned at sea. Mr Haggard had been younger than Uncle Abe when he died, but he had been a big, brawny man too, with flaming red hair.

She said, 'In that case, you'd better remember to put on a clean shirt when you get up in the morning. And wash your neck thoroughly and clean your nails. They look as if they could do with it.'

She spoke to Uncle Abe in the same sharp, almost angry way that she spoke to the children but Uncle Abe didn't mind because he was used to it.

John had the bunch of keys fastened to his belt. They were all wearing the dirty old clothes they had worn the day before but they couldn't get into the passage until Aunt Mabel was out of the house.

They thought she would never go. Usually she went shopping as soon as breakfast was cleared away but today she had taken it into her head to turn out one of the kitchen cupboards and put clean paper on all the shelves. John and Mary hung around, trying to hurry her up by helping her, but she seemed maddeningly slow, taking down each piece of china from the top shelf and wiping it carefully before she put it back again.

Mary said, 'Aunt Mabel, you really ought to get out in the open air. It's good for you.'

From her perch at the top of the step ladder, Aunt Mabel looked down at Mary's pink face.

'Well,' she said. 'Since when have you been interested in my health, may I ask?'

John said innocently, 'We've been thinking you looked a bit peaky, Aunt Mabel.'

Aunt Mabel gave a funny little snort. 'I'll go out when I'm good and ready. Not before. I've got a lot to do because it's Lifeboat Day tomorrow and I shall be busy selling flags.'

'To pay for the new Lifeboat? The one that's down on the front, near the pier?'

Aunt Mabel nodded. 'It isn't fitted out yet, though. We shall need to collect a lot of money.'

'Will you be out selling flags *all day* tomorrow?' John asked eagerly. He grinned at Mary, whose eyes shone. They could only get into the passage when Aunt Mabel wasn't there and even if she went shopping she might easily get back before they did and find out what they were doing. If she was going to be out all day, tomorrow would be a wonderful opportunity.

'Most of the time, I expect,' Aunt Mabel said. She gave them a small smile. 'As a matter of fact, I thought you might like to help ...'

'*Oh*,' said John and Mary together. Their response was hardly enthusiastic and Aunt Mabel looked at their crest-fallen faces in surprise. Although she believed they were spoiled, she had almost without realizing it, come to think of Mary and John as very helpful children who were usually willing to do things for people. She said, rather crossly, 'Well – we'll talk about it tomorrow. I'm sure *I* don't want to make you do anything you don't want to do.'

Mary said quickly, 'It's not that we don't want to, Aunt Mabel. We didn't mean ...'

'Never mind what you meant,' Aunt Mabel said. 'I'm

too busy to talk about it now. Run along and play – and take Ben with you. What's Ben doing?'

'Sitting with Miss Pin,' John said, with a little sigh.

Ben had been with Miss Pin for the last hour. She was talking about Aunt Mabel. The oil stove threw a yellow, feathery pattern on the high, dim ceiling; Ben sat close to its lovely warmth, on the leather footstool, and listened. From time to time, he fed the tortoise, Sir Lancelot, with a piece of fresh lettuce.

Miss Pin was saying, 'You should have seen your Aunt Mabel when she was young. She was the prettiest girl in Henstable. Tall and bonny, with long, graceful legs, like a deer. I used to sit here, in this room – it was just after my arthritis had laid hold of me properly – and listen to her, singing in the big garden next door. She sang all day, such sweet, pretty songs, to amuse her little sister. That was your Dear Mamma, Ben. I never saw any two sisters so loving. When your Aunt Mabel was married, your Mamma was her bridesmaid, in a pretty dress of white lace. They asked me to the wedding – such a pretty card, with gold bells all over it. Of course I couldn't go. Even if it hadn't been for my arthritis, it wouldn't have been Safe. I daren't leave Papa's treasure, you see. I'd promised him I would guard it always. But your Aunt Mabel came in to see me afterwards and brought me a piece of wedding cake. I've still got it somewhere – in that old chest in the corner, I think. She was wearing such a pretty dress ...'

'Get on to the sad bit,' Ben said. He was much more interested in hearing how Mr Haggard's ship had gone down in a great storm in the Pacific Ocean, than he was in the dress Aunt Mabel was wearing when she got married.

Miss Pin frowned. 'Don't be impatient, boy. All in good time. Just fill my kettle first, will you, dear?' She waited while Ben put a kettle on the oil stove and gave her a new one for her lap. Then she put her hat straight on her head, tucked her bright shawl firmly about her, and went on. 'For about a year, Ben dear, your Aunt and her nice young husband were happy as the day is long. My Dear Mamma used to say you can only have so much happiness in this life. Your Aunt Mabel had it all – in one short year.'

She sighed deeply, but Ben knew she was enjoying herself. Like Ben, Miss Pin thought sad things were more interesting than happy ones. She huddled up in her chair, looking like an aging parrot, and went on in a low, trembling voice. 'It came to an end so suddenly. That terrible storm at sea – I can see it, Ben. The great, purple waves breaking over the ship, the fierce winds buffeting it, the poor sailors ... The storm only lasted about an hour, but long before it was over, all was lost. They sent out S.O.S. messages, but there was no ship near enough to help them. The ship broke up completely, and went down with the brave Captain standing on the bridge, saluting. The crew took to the boats, but no lifeboat could last in that sea. No one was saved except the ship's cat who came floating ashore at some island or other, riding on an old plank and miaowing like a banshee. Just think, Ben! Your poor Aunt had only been married a year.' Miss Pin raised a corner of her shawl to her eyes as if to wipe away a tear. 'Until fourteen years ago, she was the merriest creature you ever saw. Then, suddenly, everything changed. In one month – one short month, Ben, her poor husband died and she lost her little girl. Of course your Mamma was still with her, to comfort her, but she wasn't there long. *She* married just after – out of the schoolroom ...'

'Lost *what*?' Ben interrupted her in an astonished voice. This was part of the story he hadn't heard before. 'I didn't know Aunt Mabel had a girl.'

'Indeed she did. The prettiest little thing. Very delicate, of course – like a little doll. Your Aunt and your Mamma were living in the big house next door – their parents were dead long since, you know – and your Aunt put the dear baby out in her pram while she got ready to go shopping. When she came out, the child was gone.'

Ben's eyes were large and round as saucers. He whispered, 'Did the Enemy take it? The baby, I mean?'

Miss Pin looked at him. There was a queer, sharp look in her boot-button eyes. She said slowly, 'I suppose he did, Ben dear. But I shouldn't have told you. Mrs Haggard will be cross with me.'

'Her bark is worse than her bite,' Ben said kindly. 'But you needn't worry. I won't tell her I know.'

He was going to ask Miss Pin if Aunt Mabel hadn't looked for her lost baby and why the police hadn't found it, but just at that moment the door opened a crack and John's face peered through it.

He said, in a carrying whisper, 'Ben, she's gone out. Hurry ...'

Ben stood up. 'I've got to go now, Miss Pin. Thank you for having me,' he said politely.

'It's been a pleasure, Mr Mallory,' she said in her queenly way. 'I shall be delighted to see you again. Have you still got the little horse?'

Ben dived into his pocket and brought out some rubber bands, a mint toffee that he had half sucked and put back in its paper, a nail or two and the green horse.

'What do you call him?' Miss Pin asked.

'I call him Pin,' Ben said, rather shyly. He was afraid she might not like this.

But she didn't seem to mind. Her black eyes snapped and she said, 'Guard him well. He is part of my Papa's Treasure. He will bring you luck.'

*

This time, the passage did not seem nearly so dark, nor so long. In case the torch gave out, they had bought a new battery with half a crown John had found in the pocket of his best suit. And Mary had a wet flannel, rolled in a polythene bag and stuffed under her jersey. 'We can't go into someone else's house with our hands all dirty,' she explained.

So before they tried to open the door at the head of the stairs, they stood in the cellar of the next door house and solemnly tried to clean up their faces and hands by the light of the torch. The result was rather streaky and the flannel looked very black indeed. Mary put it back in the polythene bag and left it by the cellar steps. Then she ran up to stand behind John while he tried to open the door.

It wasn't as quick and easy a business as they had expected. There were a great many keys in the big bunch, but none of them seemed to fit. John didn't say anything, but his face began to lose its cheerful expression and became determined and sad as he went on, trying one key after another.

'We could saw the door down,' Ben suggested. 'There's an old saw in our cellar.'

'Don't be silly,' Mary said crossly. 'You can't damage someone else's house. You'd be a kind of burglar.'

'Well, we are burglars, aren't we?' Ben said, looking at her with such an innocent-pretending smile on his face that she could have pushed him down the stairs.

She set her lips and said, 'Not really. I mean, we're not going to steal anything. And it isn't as if anyone lived here. We can't be doing any *harm*.'

John said in a despairing voice, 'There's no point in talking about it because it doesn't look as if we're going to get in.'

Suddenly, he threw the bunch of keys away from him and they landed with a crash in the middle of the cellar floor. He stumped past Mary and Ben to pick them up and then stood, staring in front of him with misery written all over his face.

Mary went down to him. 'Have you tried them all?' she asked. It made her feel sad inside to see John looking so unhappy. She knew that although she wanted to get inside the house, she didn't want it as badly as John did. She put her hand on his arm and he looked at her with a shaky little smile and said, 'It's horrid, isn't it? But I suppose it was nice *thinking* we might be able to see inside. It was better than nothing.'

Ben said, from the top of the stairs, 'But the door's not locked at all!'

They looked up and saw a crack of light at the top of the steps. The crack widened and they saw Ben's figure outlined against the crack from the opening door.

'But it *was* locked. I'm sure it was locked,' John cried.

'Well, it isn't now,' Ben shouted back impatiently. 'Come on. It's your old house, John. Don't you want to go first?'

John made a funny, choking sound in his throat and was up the stairs in two long leaps. He rushed through the door but once he was over the threshold he suddenly stopped, so that Ben bumped into him.

'*Ouch*,' he said.

John turned on him. 'Ssh. Don't make such a noise.'

'I couldn't help it,' Ben grumbled. 'I banged myself on the nobbles of your spine. You're so *thin*.' He was rubbing his poor nose and his eyes were watering.

'Sorry,' John said. 'But I just . . . I just feel we shouldn't rush and shout and bang about. The . . . the house mightn't like it. It's been shut up so long that it isn't used to a lot of noise . . .'

He had such a solemn look on his face that Mary and Ben did as he said, walking behind him on tiptoe and speaking in whispers. And, as a matter of fact, once they had come out of the ice-cold, bare old kitchen into which the cellar door had opened, they walked quietly and spoke in hushed whispers quite naturally.

It was such a very splendid house. It was cold as a tomb and dark because most of the curtains were drawn but once their eyes got used to the dimness they could see that the rooms were full of beautiful things. There were deep, soft carpets on the floor; in the wide hall there was even a carpet hanging on the wall, fine and soft and patterned with glowing red and gold colours. There were gold cabinets full of delicate china birds and shepherdesses and shelves that reached up to the ceilings full of old, beautiful books, and statues standing in the hall and on slender, marble columns in the big drawing room, and pictures – pictures on all the walls. Some of them were small and full of light, dancing colours and some were large and dark, in heavy carved gold frames. There was a picture of a boy in a dark velvet suit holding a dove on his wrist that Mary felt she could look at for ever and ever, and one of a man in a great, scarlet cloak, sitting on a proud, white horse. John stood in front of this picture for a long time. 'The man's eyes are so sad,' he said. 'It makes me feel funny – sort of sad and happy at the same time.'

They went into all the rooms downstairs and then climbed to the first floor up a wide, curving staircase. The bedrooms were all very big and full of pictures like the rooms downstairs and had high, old-fashioned beds with curtains hanging round them. Ben tugged at one of the curtains and a little shower of dust fell. 'No one's slept here for ages,' he said.

'Of course they haven't,' Mary said. 'Mr Reynolds – the old man the house belongs to – hasn't been here for years.'

'Two years,' John said. 'That's what Aunt Mabel told me. Can you imagine anyone having a lovely house like this and all these pictures and just *leaving* it?' He stared round wonderingly at the room they were in, which was very pretty with blue, velvet curtains at the windows and a black and gold cabinet with glass doors that had a collection of small ornaments inside. Ben went up to the cabinet and pressed his nose against the glass. 'They're like Miss Pin's,' he said. 'Look Mary – there's a little horse like mine, it's exactly the same colour.'

'It *looks* the same,' Mary agreed. 'But it can't be, quite. These must be very valuable things. That's why they're all locked up.'

'My horse is valuable too,' Ben muttered mutinously. 'And I think he's prettier,' He took out Pin and fondled him lovingly.

'He *is* pretty,' Mary said consolingly. 'But he can't be so precious. Otherwise Miss Pin wouldn't have given him to you.'

Ben said nothing but scowled at her fiercely and stumped up the next flight of stairs, glowering and dragging his feet.

There was a bathroom on the next floor with a big marble washstand and an enormous bath that had four gold lion's paws for feet. There were more bedrooms, but they were not so big and grand as the ones on the first floor, and the furniture was plainer. At the corner of the landing there was a door; John opened it and they saw a narrow flight of stairs, curving up round and round, as if it led up a tower. There was no carpet on the stairs and though the wall had been painted, it must have been a very long time ago because the paint was peeling off and there were holes in the plaster; in one place a big piece had fallen down and the laths were showing through. They climbed up, round and round, until the backs of their legs felt tired. Then, quite suddenly, the stairway took a final twist and they found themselves standing in a pool of brilliant sunlight that made them blink.

'It's the attic,' John cried in a high, excited voice.

They were at the very top of the house, in a big, long room with sloping ceilings and a wide window through which the dusty shafts of sunlight streamed. It was a bare, neglected place; there was worn, green lino on the floor and several panes of glass were missing from the windows. The corners of the ceiling were grey with cobwebs. There was a dusty chest standing under the window and against one wall there was an old brass bedstead. It had a thin mattress that was half hidden by a red silk shawl with bright coloured birds embroidered on it. The shawl had been arranged carefully over the mattress as if to cover it up as much as possible.

Mary stared and stared at the bedstead. Her breath came very fast and she was suddenly so excited that she could hardly speak.

She said in a choking voice, 'That must be the bed Aunt Mabel was talking about. The one she and mother used to play on. Do you remember? She told us about it in the train – she said it might still be here.'

'I wonder,' John said. 'I wonder . . .' He went up to the bed and touched the silk shawl. It made him feel queer to think of his mother and Aunt Mabel being young and playing games on this old bed. His face was very grave. He said, 'Perhaps no one has been up here since Aunt Mabel went away. That would be years and years . . .'

'Fourteen years,' Ben said suddenly.

'How do you know?' Mary asked.

Ben shrugged his shoulder. 'I just do.'

Mary and John looked at each other. They saw Ben was annoyed about something so it was no good trying to make him explain how he knew.

'Aunt Mabel said she sold the house after her husband died,' John said slowly. 'Perhaps that *was* fourteen years ago. It's an awfully long time. I wonder if we're the first people to come here – in all these years.'

'Of course we aren't, stupid,' Ben said.

'We *might* be,' Mary said. 'After all, if Mr Reynolds had come up here and seen what a nice room it is, he'd have painted it up and hung pictures in it.'

'Perhaps he didn't think it was nice,' John said. But that didn't seem likely, because it *was* a nice room, sunny and bright, with a friendly feeling to it. The window was high up in the roof and when John and Mary stood on the oak chest, they found they could see the sea, just as Aunt Mabel had said. It was very dark blue; the sun, shining on it, made sparkles of light that were so bright it almost hurt to look at them. John and Mary stood in silence, watching the sea-gulls and a tiny steamer, moving slowly across the horizon. After a little, John said, 'It's lovely here. Mr Reynolds can't have seen how lovely it is – he can't have come up here at all.'

'Someone else has been up here, though,' Ben said.

They turned from the window and looked at him. He was sitting on the bed, his hands in his pockets, smiling to himself.

'What do you mean?' John said.

Ben said nothing. He just whistled a little tune under his breath.

Mary sat down on the bed beside him. 'Please tell us, Ben dear,' she said pleadingly. 'I'm sorry I was rude about Pin. I think he's a beautiful horse and much nicer than the one in the room downstairs.'

Ben whistled a little bit longer. Then he relented, partly because Mary was looking at him so coaxingly, and partly because he couldn't resist showing his brother and sister how clever he was.

'You know Aunt Mabel's got some brass candlesticks in the dining room?' he said. 'Well – you know she's always polishing them. She says they go dull if you don't. *Well* –

this brass bed is all shiny and bright, isn't it? Just as if it had been polished yesterday.'

It was quite true. John and Mary were a little bit ashamed because they hadn't thought of this for themselves. 'You are clever,' Mary said.

'Yes,' Ben said smugly. He grinned so broadly that Mary thought it must make his cheeks ache. 'That isn't the only thing,' he said. 'Just *listen*.'

They listened. At first, they could only hear the singing of the birds which was very loud because the attic window was up in the roof and birds were beginning to nest under the eaves. Then they heard something else. Something so ordinary that they really hadn't noticed it. *It was a ticking clock*.

John found it. It was lying on its back on the bed, hidden under the embroidered shawl. It was a cheap-looking alarm clock with a fat, loud tick.

Ben said triumphantly, 'You see? That sort of clock has to be wound up every day.'

Mary said, 'Perhaps we jogged it – perhaps we sort of jogged it when we sat down on the bed and it started going by itself . . .'

John shook his head. 'No,' he said. 'No. It must have been wound up.' His eyes blazed bright. 'Someone *must* have been here,' he said.

5. 'Someone is Watching Me'

'I'm sure *Ben* did it,' Mary said that night after they had gone to bed and Ben was fast asleep and snoring a little because he had adenoids – so the doctor said – in his nose. 'Of *course* he did. He probably saw the clock and wound it up while we were looking out of the window, just to tease us. It's the sort of thing he *would* do.'

She was pretending to sound cross but she was secretly relieved that she had thought of such a sensible explanation. Mary was a very down-to-earth person who did not like mysteries, or, indeed, anything fanciful: she had always disliked fairy stories, for example, and much preferred to read about real people to whom real things happened.

John was quite different. He was too old to believe in fairies, but anything queer and unexplained fascinated him. He liked to lie awake in the dark and tell himself ghost stories; sometimes he frightened himself quite badly, but it was a nice, exciting kind of fear. He had been thrilled by the thought that someone might have been hiding in the House of Secrets – perhaps a fugitive from justice – and although he knew that what Mary said was probably true, that the ticking clock had just been one of Ben's tricks, he suddenly felt rather depressed all the same. He thought that Mary often made vague, mysterious things seem very ordinary and dull. He said, with a little sigh, 'Did he really have time? We only looked out of the window for a minute.'

'Ben's very quick and sort of neat, like a cat,' Mary said. 'And he probably wanted to get his own back because I'd said his horse wasn't valuable.'

John thought for a minute. Then he said, 'But he didn't have time to polish the brass bedstead, did he?' and laughed, feeling rather pleased.

But Mary had an answer to this too. 'I asked Aunt Mabel about brass. She doesn't polish everything – there's a coal scuttle in the dining room and a brass jug in the hall. And she said all brass didn't have to be polished, sometimes it has a kind of varnish on it so it can stay bright for years.' She stopped, feeling rather sorry and ashamed. She knew John liked to make up stories in his head and that she often spoiled them by being too matter-of-fact, but she also knew that she was made that way and couldn't help it. 'I'm sorry,' she said in a small voice.

'It doesn't matter,' John said. He was silent for a bit and then he said, 'I mean it *really* doesn't matter. It's just as exciting even if there's no one else there. It's secret – no one wants that old attic. We can go there whenever we like and make it our own private place. No one will know we're there.'

'We'll have to be careful,' Mary warned him. 'Aunt Mabel's got eyes in the back of her head.' She giggled, thinking of two spare eyes peeping out through the untidy mess of Aunt Mabel's grey hair. 'We could clean it up – I suppose we can't wash anything because the water must have been turned off – but we could find a broom – there must be one somewhere – and sweep the dust up. And I could paint some pictures if Uncle Abe will let me have some paints, and hang them on the walls.'

John said eagerly, 'And we could take some food – sausages and things – and cook them. Uncle Abe's got a little primus stove in his shed. He doesn't use it and it's almost rusted up, but we could drag it through the passage and make it work. And even if there isn't any water in the taps we could fill up one of those old lemonade bottles in the cellar and take that . . .'

He yawned, not because he wasn't interested in the plans he was making, but because he was simply too tired to stay awake much longer. 'We could polish up that old grate in the corner – we might even light a fire – and perhaps we could borrow a rug to put in front of it. There are so many rugs all over the house, no one could mind if we just borrowed *one* . . . It'll be such fun, won't it?' he murmured drowsily, 'such fun . . .'

Mary didn't answer because she was already asleep.

They woke up the next morning, their heads full of ideas as if their brains had been working all the time they were asleep. John was going to collect some nails from the cellar, and some pieces of wood to make shelves so that they would have somewhere to put books, when they had books; Mary decided to ask Aunt Mabel if she had any old pieces of material that she could stuff with rags and make into cushions. If the oak chest was polished up and had cushions on it, and there were bookshelves in the corner, the attic would look beautifully bright and comfortable. As for food – it would be unfair to take anything out of the larder, but it would be quite all right if they each saved something from their breakfast, a piece of bread or a sausage or something. 'Just something that we would have eaten anyway,' John explained. 'So it doesn't cost Aunt Mabel anything extra.'

It seemed more sensible not to tell Ben anything until breakfast was over and Aunt Mabel had gone out to sell flags for Lifeboat Day. Although Ben was quite good at keeping secrets he was only young. Snatching food from the breakfast table would make him excited and giggly; he might easily give the whole show away.

They had quite forgotten that Aunt Mabel had asked them to help her on Lifeboat Day and she didn't mention it. But when they were halfway through breakfast – just as John had managed to slip a beef sausage into the pocket of his shirt – Uncle Abe appeared in the kitchen.

'I want some volunteers,' he said in a loud voice.

The children looked up from their plates and stared.

He looked quite extraordinary. He was wearing a long, pale green tunic fastened at the waist – or where his waist would have been if he had one – by a broad, golden belt. His big, freckled arms were bare, so were his enormous, pale feet. On his head he wore a curious, green head-dress with pieces of real seaweed pinned on to it, and in one hand he held what looked like a huge, three-pronged fork. He grinned at the children a little sheepishly. 'I'm supposed to be Neptune,' he said. 'This is my Trident.' He waved it in the air and gave a short laugh. 'Well – what d'you think of the outfit, eh?'

The children were silent for a moment. Their faces had gone pink and John's cheeks looked strangely puffed out and tight as a balloon. Finally Mary spoke, in a funny, prim sort of voice because she was trying so hard not to laugh. 'I think you look very nice, Uncle Abe,' she said.

John made an extraordinary sound, like a bursting paper bag. Then he got up from the table and rushed headlong from the room. They heard him clatter down the passage towards the garden, whooping with hysterical laughter.

Uncle Abe drew his brows together. 'Well,' he said. 'I knew this rig didn't exactly suit my figure but I didn't think I looked as funny as all that. Dignified, that was the effect we were aiming at. Dignified and striking.' At that moment, Aunt Mabel came into the kitchen, carrying a large paper parcel. Uncle Abe said to her, 'It doesn't look, you know, as if I'm going to be quite the attraction we thought. Looks as if it might have quite the opposite effect, in fact. Young

John has just rushed intemperately from the room.' He looked at Aunt Mabel hopefully. 'Shall we call the whole thing off? I don't mind making a first class fool of myself – I'm not complaining about that – but we don't want to drive people *away*, do we?'

'You won't do that,' Aunt Mabel said calmly. 'You look very . . .' She paused and looked at Uncle Abe consideringly. 'Very – er – suitable,' she finished.

Ben said suddenly, 'What did he mean about volunteers?'

Aunt Mabel gave him a quick little smile. 'We're having a ceremony, Ben,' she said. 'We want to get as much money as possible for the Lifeboat. So we're having a band, and Uncle Abe is going to sit in a boat at the end of the jetty and when the band strikes up, he's going to get out of the boat and walk up the jetty . . .'

'Neptune, rising from the sea,' Uncle Abe said in a sad, resigned voice. 'Striking terror into the hearts of the young men and maidens. An imaginative lot, the Lifeboat committee.' He sighed deeply and rolled his eyes up to the ceiling.

'. . . and he is going to have two attendant Sea Sprites,' went on Aunt Mabel firmly. 'They were to have been the grocer's little boy and girl, but unfortunately they have German measles.' She put the brown paper parcel down on the end of the table, unwrapped it, and shook out two filmy green tunics. She held them up thoughtfully. 'I should think they will fit Mary and Ben quite nicely.'

'ME,' Ben said in a horrified voice. 'ME. You mean I'VE got to wear a DRESS?'

Aunt Mabel nodded. 'They're a bit thin and transparent. You'll have to wear a petticoat under them.'

'PETTICOAT?'

'Yes. And a good warm vest underneath so you don't catch cold.'

'VEST?' Ben said. Uncle Abe winked at him but Ben didn't smile.

Aunt Mabel said, 'Yes, Ben. Tunic, petticoat and vest. You'll be warm and you'll be pretty.'

'PRETTY,' Ben shouted. His face was so red and disgusted that Mary almost laughed although she really felt rather sorry for him: most boys hate dressing up but Ben hated it more than most.

She said soothingly, 'Perhaps you can have seaweed in your hair. And a trident, like Uncle Abe. Then everyone will see you're a *boy* sea sprite.'

Ben looked at Aunt Mabel with deep suspicion. 'Can I have a trident?' he asked.

'You can have mine,' Uncle Abe said quickly. 'You can be my Bearer.'

'It's an awfully Good Cause,' Mary said. 'It's to help all the poor sailors who might drown at sea.' She glanced shyly at Aunt Mabel as she said this, afraid that it might make her unhappy. But Aunt Mabel was looking just as she usually did: poker-faced and a little cross.

Ben said nothing for a minute. He just glowered round the room, his lower lip stuck out. Then he drew a deep breath and said, very unenthusiastically, 'All right. I don't mind.'

Mary gave a little sigh of relief. Once Ben had made up his mind, he stuck to it. He didn't look exactly happy – his grim, resigned expression suggested a Roman Gladiator facing certain death in the arena – but he stood quite still while Aunt Mabel dressed him up in the tunic and tied a gold sash round his waist and pinned a few strands of seaweed in his tousled, dark hair. Then he sat glumly in a chair and watched Mary change into her costume.

Mary enjoyed dressing up. It was a pity that the expedition to the House of Secrets would have to be put off for another day but by the time she had fastened the gold belt round the filmy green dress she had quite forgotten her disappointment and was feeling very cheerful and happy. Mary liked pleasing people and it would please Aunt Mabel if she and Ben helped to collect a lot of money for the Lifeboat. She spread out her skirts and danced round the room. 'Do I look all right, Aunt Mabel?' she said.

Aunt Mabel looked at her smiling face. 'Very pretty,' she said. 'Pretty as a picture.' She swallowed and added, in an odd voice, 'You need something for your hair. I won't be a minute.'

When she had gone out of the room, Ben said, 'Why don't you paint a picture of Mary, Uncle Abe. Aunt Mabel says you used to paint pictures.'

'I did once.' Uncle Abe gave one of his deep, gusty sighs.

'Did you sell them? That's what you do with your statues, isn't it?'

Uncle Abe grinned. 'I *try* to sell them. But does anyone *buy* them? That's the point.'

'I thought that's why you went up to London yesterday,' Ben said.

Mary frowned at him; she thought it was rude of Ben to be so inquisitive. But Uncle Abe didn't seem to mind. He just shrugged his big shoulders and said cheerfully. 'That's right. But it was a fruitless errand, as they say.' He scowled at Ben in his mock-fierce way. 'Take my advice, my boy, and learn a good trade. Be a plumber or a greengrocer.'

'I'm going to be a man in a Bank,' Ben said promptly. 'Because they always have money.' He thought for a minute and added, 'Couldn't we collect money? Like we're going to collect for the Lifeboat – only we could collect just for ourselves?'

Uncle Abe regarded him thoughtfully. 'We might, at that. We could dress you up in rags and old newspapers and stand you on the pavement with a notice. "Starving Family to Support." How would that do, eh?'

Ben's eyes gleamed. 'I could cover my face with powder so I'd look pale and sick and go without shoes. I could paint my feet with red paint, so it would look like blood – as if I'd cut my poor feet on the hard stones.'

'Fine,' Uncle Abe said approvingly. 'You've got a flair, Ben. The right touch of inspired imagination. You'll go far.'

Ben looked pleased and Mary said quickly, 'Oh *don't* Uncle Abe. If you say things like that he'll think you mean it and he'll go and do it – he'll go and collect money and then the police might come and he'd get into dreadful trouble.'

'I would not,' Ben said crossly. 'If I saw a policeman come I'd run. I'd run so fast he couldn't catch me.'

'Not in bare feet you wouldn't,' Uncle Abe said. 'Mary's right, Ben. Begging isn't thought a respectable profession in England.' He laughed loudly, wiping his eyes, and when Aunt Mabel came back she eyed him suspiciously. 'What's the joke?' she asked.

Uncle Abe hiccoughed. 'Not one you'd enjoy, Mabel. Isn't it time we were off?'

'Yes. In a minute. Come here, Mary,' Aunt Mabel said, her voice soft and her hands gentle as she smoothed Mary's hair back from her forehead and showed her a little pearl band. The pearls were sewn on black velvet stretched over a stiff frame. 'To keep your hair back,' Aunt Mabel said. 'You can keep it, afterwards.'

Mary thought it was the prettiest thing she had ever seen. She drew a deep, happy breath. 'Oh, Aunt Mabel, it's *lovely*.' She stood still while Aunt Mabel fitted it over her head and then stepped back to look at her, with a queer, thoughtful expression in her eyes.

'Was it yours, when you were a girl?' Mary asked. 'It *is* nice of you to give it to me.' She felt awkward and shy suddenly and said, 'Thank you – oh thank you,' under her breath.

Aunt Mabel said, 'Yes, it was mine. But there's no need to thank me. It's only an old thing I hadn't any use for. Come on – it's time we were off. I don't know what John's doing. I found him skulking in the garden – I told him to keep an eye on Miss Pin.'

'Here's your Trident,' Uncle Abe said to Ben. 'Carry it over your shoulder. And try to look as if you were enjoying yourself.'

Ben looked at him in disdain and made no reply.

John waited for about half an hour after the others had gone partly because of Miss Pin and partly because he wanted to savour the thought that he would soon be in the House of Secrets, all alone. John had always found that almost the best part of doing something was the excitement of thinking about it beforehand. His heart thumped away inside him all the time he was looking after Miss Pin, taking her the warm milk she always had at ten o'clock and the chopped lettuce and sliced banana for Sir Lancelot. Miss Pin didn't talk to John as she talked to Ben but treated him as a kind of servant; when he had finished filling her kettles she said, 'You may go now,' in a very grand, regal way.

But John didn't go. He stood by the door where she couldn't see him and waited until he heard a little, fluttery, snoring sound. Then he peeped round the clothes-horse that screened her and saw she was asleep. She would sleep like this, huddled up small in her gay shawl, the feathered hat nodding on her head, until lunch time. John went out, very quietly, and closed the door.

He didn't take any of the things with him that he had

planned to take. It would be more sensible to put up the bookshelves another time, when Mary and Ben would be there to help him. He thought he might look for a rug to put in front of the fireplace and perhaps find a broom to sweep up the attic, but first of all he just wanted to be there, by himself, looking at the sea from the window and thinking his own thoughts without anyone bothering him.

John never minded being alone. In a queer way, he was much less nervous of strange and lonely places when he was by himself; as he climbed the big, dark staircase of the house next door, he thought that if there were ghosts – as there well might be in this old house – he wouldn't mind at all. He would creep quietly past without disturbing them, just as if he were a ghost himself.

He didn't go into any of the rooms. He went straight up to the sunny attic, climbed on to the oak chest and pushed open the creaky old window. It was a warmer day than usual and the air felt soft and fresh. It was very enclosed up here with the old roof slanting up on either side of the window, and very private. John liked the feeling that he was shut right away from the world and that no one knew where he was.

He stood on the chest for a long time, blinking drowsily like an owl in the sun. He thought that if Mary and Ben were here, they wouldn't let him be so lazy and quiet. They would be talking loudly and wanting to do things. He sighed a little and began to feel guilty. When they knew he had spent the morning in the attic, they would expect him to have cleaned up a bit or done something to make it look nice and homely.

He wondered if there would be anything inside the oak chest that would do to furnish the attic. The lid was heavy and creaked as he opened it and a strong, musty smell came from the inside.

It seemed to be full of old clothes – several pairs of dark trousers and two jackets with gold buttons and gold trimmings – and some bundles wrapped up in newspaper. John unwrapped one of the bundles and found an old tweed hat with a label fastened on to the side with a pin. The label said, 'Father's gardening hat'. It was a very old hat with moth holes in it – a funny thing to keep so carefully wrapped up, John thought. In another newspaper bundle he found a pair of girl's satin slippers, dirty white with tarnished buckles on the front. He put the slippers and the hat back in their newspaper wrappings, lifted out the trousers and the jackets and found, at the bottom of the chest an odd mixture of things: a wooden box with chess men in it, a packet of seeds, an old hammer and a photograph album tied up with a red ribbon.

John untied the ribbon and opened the album. The photographs were rather brown and faded, and showed stiff looking people in old-fashioned clothes. As he turned the pages, the photographs became less faded and the clothes the people were wearing were much more modern. There was a photograph of two girls, one tall and frowning, one short and plump and smiling. Underneath was written, *Mabel and Hetty*. John stared at the picture; then, suddenly, his heart seemed to jump right up into his throat. Hetty was his mother's name. It gave him a very strange feeling to see what she looked like as a little girl, with a short dress and bows in her hair. Slowly, he turned over more pages but there were no more pictures of his mother. There was one of Aunt Mabel in a long white dress, holding a bouquet of flowers and several of a big, smiling man in naval uniform. The last page of the album was torn a little and looked as if someone had torn out a photograph rather roughly – a corner had been left behind. John wondered who it was a photograph of and what had happened to it. He closed the album and looked inside the chest. He found it in a corner, screwed up and squashed with all the things that had been lying on top of it. He smoothed it out on his knee and looked at it carefully. It was a picture of Aunt Mabel – a young, pretty Aunt Mabel whose hair was short and curly instead of scragged back from her face. She was smiling and holding a tiny baby wrapped in a lacy shawl.

John wondered who the baby was and thought, perhaps it was himself. He had been born in England and Aunt Mabel had known him when he was small. But why had she torn the photograph out of the album and left it loose in her chest? He knew now that this must be Aunt Mabel's chest. She had packed all these things away in it and left them behind when she sold the house and no one had touched them since. The jackets with the gold buttons must have been her husband's naval uniform; the gardening hat probably belonged to her father. Perhaps she had wanted to keep it, when he died, to remember him by.

John put the things back in the chest, folding the clothes as carefully as he could. He put the photograph of Aunt Mabel and the baby in his trouser pocket; he thought Ben and Mary would be interested to see it. When he had closed the lid, he suddenly felt rather lonely and miserable. For the first time that morning he wished that Mary and Ben were with him and he decided that he would go back home to wait for them.

He went slowly down the attic stairs and opened the door on to the top landing.

And then he stopped, holding his breath.

He could hear something: a slow pretty tune that seemed to float gently up the dark stair well to where he was standing. Someone, somewhere in the house, was playing a piano. There *was* a piano, he remembered, in one of the big rooms on the ground floor. But who was playing it? It couldn't be a burglar – not an ordinary burglar, anyway, because no ordinary burglar would stop to play the piano. Could it be a ghost? The tune was soft and somehow mournful; the sort of tune a ghost would play if a ghost *could* play.

For a few minutes John stood where he was, very still and quiet. Then slowly – very slowly – he began to creep down the stairs. His heart was thumping but he was more curious than frightened.

When he reached the hall, he could hear quite plainly where the music was coming from: the big room at the back where there was the picture of the man on the white horse. John went slowly to the door of this room and looked in. There was a large, gilt-framed mirror opposite the door and he could see the piano reflected in it and the person who was playing it. It was a girl in a high-necked brown jersey; a girl with very long, straight, dark hair, a pinched, monkey-ish face and big, dark eyes, rather like Ben's. The eyes were looking at John in the mirror, but John couldn't believe she was really *seeing* him because she went on playing. But the tune got slower and slower and at last she stopped altogether and stood up.

John drew a long breath and went into the room. She was standing by the piano, facing him. She was tall – taller than he was.

'Who are you?' she said. 'I thought – I *thought* someone was watching me.'

She wasn't a ghost. Her voice was quite ordinary and she was just as nervous as John was.

He said boldly, 'Who are *you*?'

She didn't answer for a minute, but stood, looking at John and hugging her elbows as if she was feeling shivery. Then she said in a low, breathless voice, 'I am Victoria.'

6. Victoria

'What are you doing here?' John asked. Then an awful thought struck him. Since this girl was a real person and not a ghost, she probably *lived* here. 'Are you Victoria Reynolds?' he said.

She didn't answer but bobbed her head in a little, uncertain nod that made her long hair swing like a curtain on either side of her pale face. Her big, dark eyes were fixed on John just as if she was scared of him. He was puzzled for a moment. Why should she be scared, when it was *he* who had no right to be here?

He said, 'It's all right. I'm not a ghost or a burglar or anything. I'm John Mallory. Our Aunt Mabel used to live here – some of her things are still up in the old attic.'

While he was saying this, he looked at her closely. She was dressed in an old brown jersey that was torn at the elbows and a pair of faded, grey jeans. The only pretty thing she was wearing was an old-fashioned locket that hung round her neck on a thin chain. Somehow she didn't look as if she belonged here, in this rich, beautiful house.

John said shyly, 'We haven't touched anything else, or done any harm. But I'm afraid your father will be very cross with us. Mr Reynolds *is* your father, isn't he?' She said nothing, just stared at him, rather stupidly, John thought. Then he remembered that Mr Reynolds was an old man. 'Or your grandfather. Of course, he must be your grandfather . . .'

She said, with a little gasp, 'Yes – yes, he is.'

John squared his shoulders. 'I suppose you'll have to tell

him. About us, I mean. We thought the house was empty. We thought it wouldn't matter if we came in to play, if we were careful. But I'm afraid our Aunt will be very angry.' He felt suddenly very shy and nervous. 'If – if I went away *now* – perhaps you could just forget I'd been here.' He looked at her hopefully.

She said breathlessly, 'I shan't tell anyone. I don't mind your being here. As long – as long as you don't tell anyone about *me*.' She was shaking from head to foot and her thin face looked even more pinched and unhappy.

John thought she was a very mysterious sort of person. 'Why?' he asked boldly. 'I mean – it's your house, isn't it?'

She gulped as if her throat was lumpy. Then she clenched her fists at her sides and drew herself up, very straight and tall. 'Because I shouldn't be here. *He* doesn't know I am. He – he lives in London and he thinks I'm at a boarding-school.'

'Then why aren't you?' John said, surprised. 'I thought, if you were at boarding-school you had to stay there – except for holidays and things.'

She blinked at him. 'I've run away. I'm – I'm a refugee.' Her whole face brightened and she went on quickly, 'A refugee from cruelty and injustice. It's a horrible place full of horrible people and I hate it.'

John stammered with excitement. 'B-but won't they find you? I – I m-mean, if you've escaped, won't they be looking for you?'

She gave him a sly, sideways look. 'Not yet,' she said slowly. 'It's half term and everyone goes home for half term. I told them I was going to stay with my grandfather, so they won't know until Tuesday that I'm not coming back. That's . . . that's another three days.'

'How did you get it?' John asked, interested. 'The house is all locked up.'

She scowled a little. 'I've got a key to the back door.'

'But how did you get into the garden? The wall's awfully high.'

'There's a garage at the bottom of the garden and the catch on the window's broken. You can get through the window . . .'

She said this rather reluctantly. Suddenly, her scowl deepened and she glared at John in an angry, suspicious way. She burst out, 'Why do you keep asking all these questions – I think you're a *horrible* boy.'

John was amazed. Why should she mind? 'I only wanted to know,' he said.

'I don't see why,' Victoria said crossly. 'I don't see that it's any business of yours.'

'Perhaps it isn't,' John said in a huffy voice. 'All right – I won't ask you anything else.' He waited for a moment in case she wanted to apologize for being so rude, but she showed no sign of being sorry. So he said proudly, 'I think I'll go home now. And I won't come back, so you needn't worry about being asked any more old questions.'

He was halfway across the hall before she ran after him.

'Please don't go – please. I didn't mean to be cross.' She sounded rather stiff and awkward as if she wasn't used to saying she was sorry.

John said, 'I'll stay for a bit, if you like. But there's nothing wrong in asking questions. It only means you're *interested* in a person.'

She sighed. 'All right. Ask me questions if you want to.' And she stood up straight and tall as she had done earlier – rather, John thought, as if she was standing with her back to a wall and waiting to be shot.

He said, 'Why is your boarding-school so horrid? Do they beat you, or lock you up?' John knew very little about schools of any kind but his mother had once read him

Nicholas Nickleby and he thought all boarding-schools were probably like that.

'No. They don't beat me. But ...' She hesitated and then said in a rush, 'but they won't let me play the piano. It's the only thing I like doing and they won't let me do it. They don't like me and I *hate* them.' Her voice shook with sudden passion.

John said reasonably, 'If it's a horrid school, why don't your mother and father take you away?'

'Because they're dead,' she said, not sadly, but coldly and bleakly as if she didn't care at all.

It made John feel very strange. He said uncomfortably, 'Why don't you tell your grandfather then?'

'*He* wouldn't care,' she said scornfully. 'He only cares about his old pictures. I hate him.'

'You seem to hate a lot of people,' John said. He thought this was rather odd and unpleasant of her. Surely there weren't *so* many nasty people about? He had never hated anybody himself, probably because everyone – except perhaps Mrs Epsom and Aunt Mabel – had always been kind and loving to *him*.

Victoria took no notice. Her face was puzzled. 'You said – in the beginning you said, "*we* thought the house was empty". Are there more of you?' She glanced round nervously as if she half-expected a horde of strange children to burst out of the dark, silent rooms.

'Only my sister and my brother,' John explained. 'And they're not here now because they've gone collecting for Lifeboat Day. I'll have to go home now because they'll be back for lunch. And Aunt Mabel will wonder where I am.'

'Oh,' she said. 'Oh.' And frowned. Then she went on in an off-hand way as if she didn't care much, one way or the other, 'Will you come back?'

'No,' John said. 'We can't.' He felt suddenly that he never

wanted to come into the House of Secrets again, partly because it was no longer a private place and partly because Victoria was such a disagreeable girl.

'Why?' she said and stared at him.

'Because it isn't our house. Of course it wasn't before, but now we know someone's here, it's different . . .'

'There's no one here but me.' In spite of her sullen expression she sounded rather forlorn as she said this.

'But I can't come back without Mary and Ben. And,' John added rather spitefully, 'you mightn't like *them*.'

She thrust her thin hands deep into the pockets of her jeans. 'I might. I – I like *you*.' The colour came up into her face and she looked almost pretty for once. She said quickly, 'It's so lonely here. I haven't got any friends. How old is your sister?'

'Mary's eleven,' John said. 'But she's very grown-up for her age.' He almost said, 'and more sensible', because he couldn't imagine Mary ever being as cross and touchy as Victoria, but he stopped himself just in time.

She said suddenly, 'Please – oh, *please* come back,' and then looked surprised, as if she didn't often say *please* to people.

He said, 'I suppose we could come after lunch.' He thought of something. 'What are you going to have to eat? There isn't any food in the house, is there?'

She turned away from him and carefully traced the pattern on the carpet with her toe. 'No,' she said in a low voice.

John said surprised, 'Aren't you hungry?' She didn't answer, and for some reason he began to feel rather suspicious. 'When did you come here? When did you run away from your school?'

She drew a deep breath and mumbled, 'Day before yesterday. I got here at night and . . . and I slept up in the attic. I found a shawl in the chest and slept on the bed . . .'

'And you wound up the alarm clock?' John said.

'It's my clock. Why shouldn't I wind it up?' She stared at him belligerently.

'No reason,' John said patiently. 'I only mentioned it because it was ticking when we found it yesterday – and you weren't here then.'

'Oh.' Her eyes looked very dark in her pale face and her breath seemed to be coming very quickly. 'No, I wasn't.' She paused as if she was trying to work something out in her mind – almost, John thought, as if she couldn't remember where she *had* been yesterday. She said rapidly, 'I went out, just for a bit. I was awfully hungry. I only had a shilling left over from my train ticket so I could only buy a carton of milk and a Crunchie Bar from the machines near the station.'

'Is that all you've had to eat? Since *yesterday*?' John was horrified. 'You must be dreadfully hungry.'

'I'm *starving*,' she said softly. 'My stomach's gone flat – look.'

She did look very thin, all bones and hollows.

John said, 'I haven't got any money to buy food. But I'll get something, I promise. And I'll bring it back this afternoon. And – and if you go up to the attic, you'll find a cold sausage on the mantelpiece. You can start on that.'

Her mouth twisted into a nervous, half-smile as if she were secretly amused about something. But she said, 'Thank you,' in a polite, if stilted way. And then she sighed a little and said, 'If you really are going, shall I let you out through the back door?'

'Yes please.' John felt relieved: not only would it be much easier to leave the house that way, but he would not have to explain how he had got in. He was surprised Victoria hadn't asked him, though. She seemed to be a remarkably uninquisitive person. Perhaps she just wasn't interested in other people.

She took him downstairs to the kitchen and out through the back door into the garden. It was a very enclosed garden, very wild and tangly as John had imagined it would be. The trees and bushes were so overgrown that they met overhead and made a dim, leafy avenue down the garden to the empty garage. The dusty window was shuggly in its frame and creaked noisily as Victoria opened it. It gave on to a short, cobbled alley with grass growing between the stones.

'Go along to the end,' Victoria said. 'Then turn left, and you'll be in the street.'

She closed the window. For a moment, her face looked out, pale and blurred behind the dirty, cobwebbed pane. Then she was gone before John could say good-bye. He walked backwards across the alley and stood for a minute, staring up at the windows of the house. They looked just as blank and empty as they had always done. No one would guess someone was hiding there.

He got home just before Aunt Mabel and the others, who came in very flushed and excited. 'Hundreds of people looked at us,' Ben said. 'Hundreds and hundreds. And they gave Aunt Mabel pounds and *pounds*. I should think she'll be able to buy a *battleship*.'

He had quite forgotten how much he had hated his costume and was even unwilling to take it off.

'Can I keep it on till after lunch?' he begged. 'I want to show Miss Pin.'

He shot off, down the passage to her room, and Mary looked at John. 'What have you been doing?' she whispered, but Aunt Mabel was standing within earshot, so he said, 'Oh – nothing. Just messing about.'

As there was no chance to take Mary into the secret, he decided it would be too difficult to take food off the table while they were having lunch. But if he ate very little himself, it would be quite fair to take something out of the larder afterwards.

'Aren't you hungry, John?' Aunt Mabel said, looking, with surprise at the minute piece of cold ham and the one, small baked potato he had put on his plate.

'Not very,' he said, eyeing the dish in the middle and calculating what he might reasonably have been expected to eat: at least one more slice of ham and two potatoes, and several pieces of bread.

Aunt Mabel frowned. 'Are you feeling all right? I thought you looked a bit pale, this morning.'

'I'm naturally a pale person,' John said. 'It's because I've got a thick sort of skin. The blood doesn't show. And I've just got a naturally small appetite.'

Mary and Ben stared at him and Aunt Mabel gave a snort of laughter. 'It's the first time I've noticed it, I must say.'

But to John's relief she seemed disinclined to say any more. She was too concerned to finish lunch and clear away so that she could go out flag-selling all afternoon. 'There's no need for Mary and Ben to come,' she said. 'They did their share this morning. So you can all do what you like – as long as you don't get into mischief. Miss Pin will be all right because a friend of mine has offered to pop in and see to her tea. If you like, you can go out and take a picnic.'

John almost jumped for joy. He had been thinking that a slice of ham and two baked potatoes would hardly be enough for someone who had only had a carton of milk and a Crunchie Bar since yesterday evening. While Aunt Mabel cut sandwiches, he stood by the table, watching her.

'I should think that will be enough,' she said, reaching for a polythene bag.

'I don't know,' John said, 'we might be awfully hungry.'

'I thought you had a naturally small appetite,' Aunt Mabel said.

'It might have got bigger by tea time. In fact I can feel it growing already.'

She looked at him with a mystified expression, then shrugged her shoulders and buttered two more slices of bread and stuck them together with marmite. 'I should think this will keep you from actual starvation,' she said drily.

As soon as she had gone, John rushed upstairs to where Ben and Mary were changing into their ordinary clothes. They could see that something had happened from the expression on his face but he didn't tell them about Victoria at first. John enjoyed telling stories and found it was always more exciting to keep the best part until the end.

'I went up into the attic,' he said slowly, 'and I opened the chest – it's full of old things that belonged to Aunt Mabel. Clothes and a photograph album. I brought one photograph with me.' He took the picture of Aunt Mabel out of his pocket. 'I think the baby must be me.'

Ben looked at the picture. 'It's not you. It's Aunt Mabel's baby!'

They stared at him. 'Aunt Mabel hasn't got any children,' Mary said.

'She *did* have. Miss Pin told me. But the baby was lost – the Enemy stole her, when she was small.'

Mary and John looked at each other. John said gently, 'I think Miss Pin sometimes gets a bit mixed up – I mean, she's old and she gets a bit muddled.'

Ben said stubbornly, 'She does *not*. She *knows*. She said

Aunt Mabel just put the baby in the pram and when she came out, it was gone.'

Mary said, 'But Ben, if someone had stolen a baby, the police would find it. Babies don't just *disappear*.'

She gave a little, disbelieving laugh that annoyed John. He hadn't believed Ben either, but now he said, 'They do sometimes. Gipsies steal children. I read a story about that once – about a girl who was really the daughter of a Duke and the gipsies stole her and brought her up.'

'Why?' said Mary flatly.

John looked at her prim, pretty face and sighed. It must be awfully dull to be Mary sometimes. He said patiently, 'I don't know. Perhaps girls are valuable. They are in Africa. African people always want to have girls because when they marry their father gets lots of cows as a bride-price.'

'I don't think that sort of thing happens in *England*,' Mary said, and put her nose in the air.

'She's awfully stupid, isn't she, John?' Ben said sweetly. 'She doesn't like to hear about exciting things.'

'I do, I *do*,' Mary protested. 'Only I like them to be *true*.'

Her lips quivered ominously and John said quickly, 'All right. If you like, I'll tell you something now. Something that's exciting *and* true.'

He paused for a minute, to make it more dramatic, and then he told them about Victoria.

They couldn't find her at first. She wasn't in the garden and though they went all over the house, calling softly, she didn't seem to be there either. John began to feel rather lost and bewildered.

'Perhaps she was a ghost after all,' he suggested, but Mary laughed.

'She left the back door open, didn't she?' she said. 'Ghosts don't unlock doors. They go *through* them.'

In the end, Ben found her, hiding behind the curtains in the piano room. He pulled them back and she stood there, red and dishevelled and scowling.

'This is my sister, Mary, and my brother, Ben,' John said politely, and she nodded coolly, her hands in the pockets of her jeans. 'We've brought you some food,' he went on. 'Ham and baked potatoes and Aunt Mabel made us a picnic tea. So you won't be hungry tonight.'

She looked at the basket but she didn't say anything. Mary thought it was rude of her not to say thank you, so she said, 'John hardly ate any lunch. So we'd have more to bring you.'

Victoria tossed her head. '*I* didn't ask him not to eat his lunch, did I?'

John said, 'It doesn't matter. I wasn't very hungry.' He could tell what Mary was thinking, from the expression on her face, and he felt ashamed because Victoria was behaving so badly. 'Do you want to eat something now?' he asked. 'Or would you rather play a game or something?'

'I don't mind,' she said.

John took the napkin off the top of the basket and gave her a sandwich and a potato. She ate slowly, watching the children warily as if she was half-afraid of them. While she was eating, Mary wandered over to the piano. 'Have you been playing?' she asked. 'Would you play us a tune?'

Victoria swallowed the last crumb of potato and went pink. 'Do you want me to?'

'Yes please,' John said. He wasn't much interested in music but he thought it might make Victoria happier if she was doing something she liked to do.

She sat down at the piano and began to play – a slow, rather grand tune that reminded the children of the sea, rolling in steadily the way it does on a calm day. As she played, Victoria stopped scowling and her thin face became absorbed and calm. She was really quite pretty, Mary thought, when she didn't look so disagreeable. The Mallorys sat down on a long, high-backed sofa that was covered with a white dust sheet and listened. At first Ben wriggled a bit – he had never listened to music before – but after a little while he sat still.

The music grew louder, as if a storm was brewing over the sea; Mary fancied that she could feel the dark clouds gathering. Underneath the top notes there seemed to be a steady, low, drumming tune that grew firmer and louder until the children felt their feet tapping as if they wanted to march.

Suddenly, Victoria stopped playing. She said, 'It's no *good*. This next bit ought to be loud and grand like . . . like trumpets blowing. And I can't play it like that because I have to keep the soft pedal down . . .' She sounded really sad – almost despairing as if it was very important to her to play the piece properly.

Mary said, 'You're awfully good. I've never heard a girl play the piano like that. Like someone in a real concert.'

'Did you like it?' Victoria smiled – it was the first time she had smiled and it made her look quite different.

'Yes,' Mary said. She remembered what a visitor had said when Sara Epsom had played for him. 'It was pretty. You must have had a lot of lessons.'

The smile went from Victoria's face – just like the sun going in on a showery day. 'I did have lessons. Then they stopped them. They said they were a waste of money.' She brought her hands down on the keys and played a loud, ugly chord. 'Beasts, *beasts*,' she said.

John said quickly, 'Play something soft – something that's meant to be soft, so it won't matter.'

She frowned for a minute and then began a light, tripping tune that was so cheerful and gay that Mary found it difficult to keep still. Her legs itched to run and jump. It seemed to affect Victoria in much the same way; when the tune was finished she said, 'I like that one. It makes me want to dance.'

'Let's have a game,' Ben said suddenly. He had liked the music but it was hard for him to sit still for long. 'My legs are tired out with sitting,' he said.

'A game?' Victoria said. 'What sort of game?'

The Mallorys looked at each other feeling rather shy and uncomfortable. It was Victoria's house and it was up to her to suggest a game. But she stood still and waited and the sullen look was beginning to come back into her face, so Mary said diffidently, 'We could play hide-and-seek.'

'Hide-and-seek?' Victoria said. 'I'm not a *kid*.'

John said, 'It should be quite good fun in this house. I mean there are lots of dark places. We could divide up into girls and boys – one pair hides, you see, and the other finds, and when you're found you have to get back to the Home – that could be the hall – without being caught.'

'All right,' Victoria said grudgingly. 'I don't mind.'

It wasn't much fun at first. Victoria had no idea how to play. Though she hid where Mary told her to she didn't try to escape when she was found, but just stood, looking wooden and awkward and as if she thought the whole thing beneath her dignity. She made John and Mary feel self-conscious and a bit silly – perhaps this was rather a babyish game, after all! Then, quite suddenly she changed; it was impossible to tell why or how. One minute she had a sneering, bored expression on her face, the next she was shrieking and careering up and down stairs, her cheeks pink and her eyes shining, as if she had been playing this game all her life. In fact, she became much noisier and rougher than the others. Once or twice she laughed so loudly that Mary was frightened. The house was solid and the walls were thick but if they made too much noise someone might hear them out in the street.

Then an awful thing happened. Victoria was racing down the stairs with Ben after her, when she tripped and stumbled against a marble column that had a Bust – a man's head and shoulders – on top of it. The column toppled over and the Bust came down and broke in pieces on the black and white marble floor of the hall.

'Oh,' Victoria said. '*Oh.*'

They were all shocked. But Victoria – Victoria was horrified. She stood and stared, her hand pressed to her mouth.

'Perhaps it can be mended,' John said hopefully, after they had stood for some time, looking at the floor in silence.

No one bothered to answer him. The Bust was broken in so many pieces that only a magician could have put it together again.

Then – this was almost more awful than the Bust being broken – Victoria began to cry. She cried with deep, silent sobs, like painful hiccoughs, that seemed to shake her whole body. She made no noise at all.

After a few minutes, John said nervously, 'Don't cry. Please, Victoria, don't cry. I know it's awful, but it was an *accident*. Your grandfather can't be *too* angry. He's got so many things.'

Victoria said, 'You don't understand – oh, you don't understand,' and sat on the foot of the stairs, a crumpled heap of misery, her long hair falling forward and covering her face. She cried so hard that Mary almost wanted to cry herself, in sympathy. Then she said, and her voice was so trembly that they could hardly hear it, 'I shall get into such a row – it's terrible – oh, I wish I was dead, I wish I was dead.'

Mary said wonderingly, 'Her grandfather must be a very angry person. A – a sort of *ogre*.' It seemed incredible that anyone could be so frightened of a relation. She drew a deep breath and sat down on the stair beside Victoria. She said, 'If – if you stop crying, I'll say it was *me* that did it.'

Slowly, Victoria lifted her head. Her eyes were red-rimmed and her poor nose pink and swollen. 'Would you really?' she said in a low, astonished voice. 'Would you really?'

Mary nodded. Her mouth felt dry. 'It won't matter – I mean he can't do anything to me.'

Victoria gave a deep sigh. Then she said, nastily, 'I don't suppose you *will* say you did it. Not when someone asks you.'

Mary gasped. 'Don't be so horrible,' John said, standing in front of them, his eyes blazing at Victoria. 'Of course Mary will say she did it – or I'll say I did. I think you're a beastly person not to believe what Mary says. Beastly and horrible.'

His face was quite as cross as Victoria's. Victoria looked at him in surprise. Then she said slowly, 'I just don't understand why she should take the blame, that's all.'

'Because she's sorry for you,' John said. 'And she's sorry for you because you're so horrid and such a beastly coward, that's why. You ought to say thank you to her at once.'

Victoria went red and then very white and her mouth looked screwed up and small. She stood up and for a second Mary thought she was going to fly at John and hit him. Then she controlled herself and said stiffly, 'I'm sorry, Mary. I'm sorry I didn't believe you. Only – only no one's ever tried to stop me getting into trouble before.'

Mary felt sorry for her, and angry with John. She said shyly, 'It's all right. Don't mention it. I – I think we ought to sweep up the pieces, don't you?'

'I'll do it,' Victoria said eagerly. 'I know where there's a dustpan and brush. Down in the kitchen.' And she ran off, down the basement stairs.

Ben sidled up to Mary and tugged her sleeve. 'I don't like her,' he said. He thought for a minute and added, 'Do you know who she looks like? She looks like Aunt Mabel.'

Mary whispered, 'I think it's only because she looks sort of sour and pinched up. She looked quite different when we were playing.'

Victoria came back then and swept up the pieces carefully. John stood the column up again but it looked queer and naked without the Bust on top of it.

'You can't help noticing it's gone,' Mary said. She thought of how angry Aunt Mabel was going to be and it gave her a hollow feeling in her stomach.

'*I* know,' Ben said. He jumped up and down with excitement. '*I* know. We can get another Bust and stick it on top. Then her horrible old grandfather won't notice.'

'How can we?' said John. 'Where'd we get one from?'

'Uncle Abe. He's got lots – he makes them to sell, doesn't he? Well, why shouldn't he sell one to us?'

'We haven't got any money,' Mary said. 'A Bust must cost pounds and pounds.'

'Easy terms,' Ben said. 'That's what it says in the shop where they sell television sets.' He had spent quite a lot of time, his soft nose squashed against the glass of the electrician's shop, watching the television on the show set in the window. The Mallorys had never seen television before because there wasn't any television in Kenya and Aunt Mabel didn't have a set, although she said she sometimes rented one for the visitors in summer. 'We could pay it off in instalments. I've got one and fourpence halfpenny,' Ben said.

'And I've got five shillings in my piggy bank,' Mary said, smiling to humour him.

John said, 'We can't afford to use that. We may need it, to buy food for Victoria.'

Mary was taken aback. John had said that Victoria was a Refugee from Injustice and that they would have to look after her and bring her food, but Mary hadn't taken this altogether seriously. Even if Victoria *had* run away from her boarding-school, she couldn't just hide, for ever. In fact, Mary had thought it was all a sort of game but now, looking at John's solemn face and remembering how frightened Victoria was of her terrible grandfather, she saw that it wasn't a game at all. Suddenly, she felt very young and scared.

John was saying, 'If we've got five shillings, we can buy milk and bread. You have to have milk for bones and teeth. And we can leave the rest of the picnic for supper and tomorrow's breakfast. And if we all –' he looked sternly at Ben, '– if we *all* try to eat a bit *less*, we can bring things from home every day.' He turned to Victoria. 'Shall you mind being in the house all night?'

She was standing with her hands behind her back, grinning nervously.

'I don't mind if . . . if . . .' She looked at the children one after the other and gabbled shyly, '. . . if you'll promise to come back tomorrow.'

'Of course we'll come back,' Ben said. 'We've got to put the Bust back, haven't we?'

After the children had left, an odd thing happened. Victoria waited in the garage until the sound of their voices and of their feet, scampering down the cobbled alley, had quite disappeared. Then she went slowly up the garden but instead of going into the house, she locked the back door and hid the key under a mossy stone. She went back to the garage – creeping through the twilit garden like a thief in the dusk – climbed out of the window and walked softly to the end of the alley. There she stopped and peered up and down the street, biting at her thumb nail. When she was quite sure the street was empty, she came out of the alley and began to run, keeping always in the shadows, towards the sea.

7. Miss Pin's Treasure

Ben was very quiet all through supper. He was thinking. He decided that it would be stupid to tell John and Mary what he was going to do because they would disapprove of it. And even if they approved, they would think it was silly. They didn't know what Ben knew. They didn't know Miss Pin was rich.

Ben was quite sure that she was as rich as she said she was. And since she was rich, there was no reason why she shouldn't lend him some money. Ben remembered his father telling him once that if you needed money badly, you could always borrow from the Bank. Ben knew he was too young for that – the Bank wouldn't lend him any money, but Miss Pin never seemed to be very sure how old people were. Certainly she never treated Ben like a boy. She always spoke to him as if he was a grown person.

After supper, he slipped out of the kitchen and went into Miss Pin's room.

She was singing a song to Sir Lancelot and feeding him with a piece of banana before she tucked him up in the box of hay where he slept at night.

'Good evening, Mr Mallory,' she said. 'Are you joining me in a game?'

They played draughts together. Ben usually won but sometimes he let Miss Pin beat him, for the sake of fairness. The happiest times came after the games, when Ben sat on the footstool and Miss Pin told him stories, and the dark, crowded room was silent except for her cracked old voice.

Ben got out the draught board and set out the pieces. He

said, 'I don't suppose I shall be able to come quite so often next week.'

'Why not?' Miss Pin asked.

'Because I shall be busy,' Ben said. 'Do you want to be white or black?'

'White. White is my lucky colour. Busy doing what?'

'Earning money,' Ben said.

Miss Pin's eyes were bright and sharp as a bird's and they watched Ben closely. 'What do you want to earn money for? I don't need to earn money. Consider the lilies of the field. They toil not, neither do they spin.'

'That's in the Bible,' Ben said. 'I just need some money. There's something I need to buy. You can start if you like.'

Miss Pin moved one of her pieces with the tip of her gloved finger. 'If you want something, why don't you ask your Aunt?'

'Because she's poor,' Ben said. 'She hasn't got any money so it would be no good asking her. Your move.'

'You're not paying attention,' Miss Pin said, and cackled with laughter. 'Look, I've taken you.' She put Ben's man down beside her. Then she said, 'I don't bother myself with household affairs but this seems to be quite a well run establishment. The standard of service isn't what it was, perhaps, and Mrs Haggard seems to have trouble with her staff. But by and large I've nothing to complain of.'

They played in silence. Ben seemed to be having bad luck, or maybe he wasn't paying attention, because Miss Pin took four of his men, one after another.

She said, 'I wouldn't have said your Aunt was poor. She is always decently clothed. Besides, poor people live in cottages.'

'Not always,' Ben said. 'In Africa, they live in mud huts.'

'There,' said Miss Pin triumphantly. 'One, two, *three*.' She placed three of Ben's men neatly on top of one another.

Ben said, 'And if people don't come and stay here, Aunt Mabel doesn't make any money. And if she doesn't make any money, we shall all starve.'

Miss Pin frowned. She said nothing, but concentrated on winning the game, which she did in two minutes flat. She sat back and said, 'Shall we have another?'

'If you like.' Ben set out the pieces again, and sighed. 'I don't really feel like playing tonight.'

Miss Pin leaned back in her chair. There was no sound in the room except the little crackle Sir Lancelot made as he moved about in the hay.

Finally Miss Pin said, 'Are you asking me for some of my Treasure, Ben?'

For once in his life, Ben felt a little nervous and strange. Miss Pin's eyes were so very bright and unwinking – and fixed on his face.

'No,' he said bravely. 'Just to borrow something. Like people borrow from the Bank. I can pay you back, bit by bit. I'm going to collect cockles on the beach like the men do. If you collect enough you can take them to the fish shop and make a lot of money.'

'Can you really?' Miss Pin said. 'What an extraordinary thing! Do you know – I used to collect cockles when I was a little girl. Dear Mama disapproved, naturally, I was always so beautifully and richly dressed. Even on the beach, I wore silken gowns and white cotton gloves.'

'You must have got them awfully messy,' Ben said and sighed a little, because once Miss Pin began to wander off into tales of her childhood, it was often difficult to bring her back again. But she was not wandering this evening. She said suddenly, 'Go over to that box in the corner, Ben. The one with the silk rug over it. It was my Papa's chest.'

Underneath the silk rug was a tin trunk with a brass lock.

'I have the key here,' Miss Pin said. She unclasped a thin

chain from round her neck. The key was warm from where it had rested against her powdery skin. Ben took it and carefully opened the trunk.

A perfumed, spicy smell came out of it – a smell that reminded Ben of Indian shops in small, African towns. The trunk was full of small objects wrapped in pieces of old, yellow silk. Exploring, Ben found some pale green animals and tiny figurines, like the things Miss Pin kept on the table beside her.

'There's a cloth bag at the side,' Miss Pin said.

Ben felt at the side of the trunk and found a bag, made of what looked like a piece of old, blue, curtain material. It was gathered tight at the neck by a red cord.

'Take it out and bring it to me,' Miss Pin said.

Ben wanted to examine the trunk, there were so many queer, pretty things in it, but her voice was so sharp and peremptory that he didn't dare. He carried the cloth bag over to Miss Pin. It was heavy and when he put it on her lap, it collapsed with a *chunk*.

She untied the red cord and shook the contents of the bag into her lap, a pile of yellow coins that looked like new halfpennies, only smaller. Not quite like halfpennies, though – more like some strange, foreign money. Miss Pin selected one and gave it to Ben.

'Here,' she said. 'I trust this will help you out of your little financial difficulty.' She scooped up the other coins with trembly, gloved hands and put them back in the bag. 'Put them back in the trunk,' she said and gave a deep sigh. 'Riches are a great responsibility, Mr Mallory. Too heavy a burden for an old woman.'

Ben put the bag in the trunk and locked it up and gave the key to Miss Pin. The little coin she had given him was hard and cold in his palm. He felt very miserable. Miss Pin hadn't understood after all. She had given him an old foreign coin that wasn't worth anything. And he couldn't tell her so because she obviously believed it was real money. Poor Miss Pin.

He said, 'Thank you very much, Miss Pin. I'll – I'll pay you back.'

'It is a Gift,' she said graciously. 'Not a loan. Neither a borrower nor a lender be. Remember that. Lending money is as bad as giving someone a knife. It cuts friendship. That is what Dear Papa said, when he was forced to leave London . . .' Her eyes were half-closed and she began to tell Ben the story she had told him before, about how her father had lent money to a friend and the friend had gone off with it, leaving them in what Miss Pin called 'very straitened circumstances'.

Ben wondered what 'very straitened circumstances' were, but he felt too depressed to ask her.

She was saying, 'But of course, we still had the Treasure. Papa would never dispose of it, though. He said it was to be my Little Capital. He was always so kind and careful of me . . .' Her voice was sleepy and her soft, pleated mouth sagged a little. Sometimes in the middle of these stories, she would drop off into a little doze, wake up a few minutes later and go on where she had left off.

But she wasn't dozing now. She said suddenly in a brisk, clear voice – quite unlike her story-telling voice – 'Benjamin, I want you to tell me the truth, now. Are you a truthful person?'

'Yes,' Ben said, rather indignantly.

'I thought you were.' The feathers bobbed on her hat as she nodded her head thoughtfully. 'Now, listen. Is your Aunt really poor?'

'Yes,' Ben said. 'We're a worry to her because we cost so much to feed.'

Miss Pin said nothing for a minute. Then, 'Ben, I want

you to do something for me. In that bureau over there you will find paper and ink. And a pen. Bring them to me.'

He opened the bureau and found a pile of mauve paper, thick and smelling of something sweet and musty, like violets. There was a thin, ivory pen-holder and a bottle of blue ink. He took them to Miss Pin and she cleared a place on the table beside her.

'Will you wait while I write a letter?' she said.

It seemed to take her a long time. Her fingers were stiff and couldn't hold the pen properly. The nib scratched and scratched, from time to time she gave a little sigh: there was no other sound in the room. When she had covered a sheet with her pointed, spidery writing, she wrote an envelope, put the letter inside and sealed it. Then she leaned back in her chair, looking crumpled and tired. She said slowly, 'I want you to post this for me. Tonight. It is a letter to a solicitor. Do you know what a solicitor is, Benjamin?'

'No,' Ben said.

Miss Pin smiled, a thin ghost of a smile. 'Never mind. You will find out, I daresay. I am tired now. Perhaps you will tell your Aunt I am ready to settle for the night.'

Her eyes drooped, she seemed almost asleep already. Ben tiptoed from the room and called down the basement stairs to Aunt Mabel. 'Miss Pin wants to settle.' Then he slipped out of the front door before she could tell him it was time for bed.

It was dark outside and raining in the wind. Ben ran to the nearest post box. There was a stamp machine beside it. Rather reluctantly he took threepence out of his pocket and got a stamp, stuck it on the envelope and posted the letter.

On the way back, he passed a lighted shop that sold tobacco and sweets. He stopped outside it and took the coin Miss Pin had given him out of his pocket. It was very pretty – bright yellow with a rough, milled edge like a half-crown and had a picture on one side of a man on a horse killing a dragon. It was almost certainly worthless. Ben thought for a minute, then made up his mind and marched into the shop.

'Can you change this?' he asked the fat woman behind the counter. 'I want a packet of mints.'

She looked at the coin he held out to her and gave a good-natured laugh. 'Bless you, no, sonny. We only take good English money in this shop.' She saw his disappointed face and added, 'Is it all you've got, love? Go on then – take a packet of mints, if that's what you want.'

'Oh, no, I couldn't do that,' Ben said. His face went pink. 'You see I have got some English money, only I don't want to spend it. It's – it's for something else.'

She laughed again, she was a very jolly, cheerful person. 'Well, I don't want your savings. Go on, have the mints. Pay me back when you've got some spare cash.' Her eyes twinkled at him and Ben thought she might be hurt if he said no. Besides, he wanted the mints.

He said politely, 'It's very kind indeed. Thank you.'

Outside the shop he opened the packet and put two mints in his mouth, one in each cheek. He sucked thoughtfully, feeling rather sad. Poor Miss Pin. She was just old and a bit muddled as John had said. And she was poor, too, like Aunt Mabel. He spun the little coin up in the air, caught it, and looked at it affectionately. It was very pretty and winked at him under the light of the street lamp. He said, 'I'll keep it always. It can be my lucky coin.' Then he ran home, whistling.

When he got back to *The Haven*, he pushed open the front door that he had left on the latch. He was very quiet, but Aunt Mabel must have heard him because she called out, 'Ben – Ben, is that you? It's bedtime.'

He screwed up his face and tiptoed, soft as a cat, down the

passage to the garden. The light was blazing in Uncle Abe's shed and Uncle Abe was working on a great slab of terra-cotta on the table.

'Uncle Abe,' Ben said, 'can I look at your things?'

Uncle Abe barely glanced at him, he was very busy. 'Look all you want to.'

Ben walked slowly round the workshop. There were little statues on all the shelves and several busts. There was one Ben liked particularly. It was the head and shoulders of an African boy who looked like Thomas. Ben examined this bust for a long time and then he said, 'Uncle Abe?'

'Mmm?'

'Uncle Abe – you do sell your things, don't you. Would you sell one to me?'

'What?' Uncle Abe swung round, his eyes wide and surprised. Then he smiled. 'Well – which one do you like?'

'This one.'

'Why?'

'It's like my friend. My friend in Africa,' Ben said.

Uncle Abe shrugged his shoulders. 'I daresay you can have it in your room, if you like. Might as well be there as here, if it takes your fancy.'

'I didn't mean that,' Ben said. 'I mean – I want it for my own. To do what I like with. I want to *buy* it.'

Uncle Abe's laugh boomed out. Then he stopped laughing and said apologetically, 'Sorry, boy. Bad-mannered of me. Well – I'm always open. What's your offer?'

Ben stood up tall, his face intent. 'I haven't got much money. But I thought, if I gave you what I had, then I could pay the rest by Easy Terms. Like you pay the television shop. I could earn money.'

Uncle Abe stroked his chin and said nothing.

Ben said desperately, 'I'd work awfully hard, I really would. I can collect cockles and run errands and ... and I could work for you if you like. I could clean out your workshop.'

'No, no,' Uncle Abe said hastily. 'Not that. But you could collect cockles, could you? Well – I daresay I owe you a bit, you've collected a good many for me.'

'Oh, no,' Ben said. 'I wouldn't want you to pay for the cockles you've *had*. They were presents. But if you liked, you could pay me for the cockles I get from now on. I'd try hard to get especially nice ones.'

'I suppose that's a fair bargain,' Uncle Abe said slowly. 'Let's say sixpence a day. Say two and sixpence a week, counting out Sundays and supposing one day to be rainy. The Bust should fetch – say seventy-five pounds. That means you'll have to collect cockles for . . . let's see . . .'

'It'll take eight weeks to collect a pound,' Ben said in a dispirited voice.

Uncle Abe looked at him admiringly. 'That's sharp. How long will seventy-five pounds take?'

Ben closed his eyes. 'Six hundred weeks. That's about twelve years.'

'Mmm. And interest, of course. Still, it depends what you've got to put down as deposit . . .'

Unhappily, Ben turned out his pockets. 'I've got one and three halfpence. I had one and fourpence halfpenny, only I had to post a letter for Miss Pin.'

Uncle Abe looked at the money, laid out on Ben's grubby palm. He cleared his throat. 'Well, that cuts it down a bit, certainly. Tell you what – I daresay I'm overcharging a bit. You usually make a special price for a friend. You collect the cockles and you can have the Bust. And when you become a wizard financier, as I daresay you will with your head for maths, you can pay off the remainder.'

Ben's face glowed. 'Here's the money,' he said. 'One and three halfpence. That's all I've got except for the lucky coin

Miss Pin gave me.' He paused and added, rather unwillingly, 'You can have that too, if you really want it. It's a foreign coin, but I suppose it would come in useful if you went abroad.'

'No, no – you keep it. Miss Pin gave it to you, did she? Getting lavish in her old age.' Uncle Abe grinned, as if this was a huge joke. 'Sure she could spare it, Ben?'

'Oh – *easily*,' Ben said. 'She's got hundreds and hundreds of coins, just like this one.'

8. 'Just a Parcel of Thieving Brats'

The next morning Victoria was waiting for them in the garden of the house next door. This time she didn't scowl. She smiled as cheerfully as anyone and said, 'I thought you were never coming.'

'We had to wait until Aunt Mabel was upstairs, doing the rooms,' Mary explained. 'Because we had to get out of the house with *this*.'

In his arms, Ben was carrying a large, roundish object, wrapped in newspaper. He held it as carefully as if it were a basket of eggs.

'What is it?' Victoria asked.

'You'll see,' Mary said mysteriously. 'You mustn't look yet. If you stay in the kitchen, we'll call when we're ready.'

They went through the kitchen, upstairs and into the hall. Ben placed his bundle gently on the floor and unwrapped it. Then John picked up the Bust of the African child, stood on tiptoe and placed it on top of the empty marble column.

'Come and see,' he called.

Victoria came into the hall and saw the Bust. She stared and stared. Her thin face grew quite fat and radiant as she smiled. 'It's beautiful,' she said in a breathless voice. 'Oh – it's a beautiful thing.' And she went on staring at it in a rapt, awestruck way that the Mallory's found a little absurd.

John said, 'I've brought you some breakfast.' He produced what he had managed to save: a boiled egg, rather squashed, and two pieces of bread and butter stuck together and a trifle hairy from John's pocket.

'I'm afraid the egg's a bit cold,' John said. 'But I

remembered to bring a teaspoon. There are some egg cups and plates in the glass cupboard in here.'

Victoria followed him into the big, gloomy dining room. She said in a shocked voice, 'But we can't use the things in that cabinet. They're *valuable*.'

Mary said, 'Surely your grandfather won't mind? Not if we're careful.'

The cupboard door was unlocked; Mary opened it and took out a very pretty plate with a pattern of green and gold leaves round the rim. She chose an egg cup with pink flowers on it and put the two pieces down on the dark, polished table. 'There,' she said. 'Sit in this big chair and you'll be like the Queen.'

'And we'll be your servants, waiting on you hand and foot.' Ben said, and giggled.

'I . . . I can't,' Victoria whispered. Her voice was so low and scared that the children looked at her curiously. She was very pale and frightened and twisting her thin hands together in front of her. Mary and John began to feel nervous themselves, but Ben, who never felt shy or awkward, said loudly, 'Don't be silly. It doesn't matter, eating off the table as long as you don't make a mess. And you're not a baby.'

'No . . .' Victoria gave Ben a tremulous smile. Then she did sit down in the chair – very cautiously, on the edge. She picked up the spoon, took the shell off the egg and began to eat. She ate slowly, not like a starving person but like someone who didn't much care for cold egg and hairy bread-and-butter. John nudged Mary and said, 'I think we'll go up to the attic. You can come when you've finished breakfast.'

While they were climbing the twisting, wooden stairs, he explained. 'It's embarrassing to be watched when you're eating.'

'She didn't look very hungry,' Ben said.

'Perhaps her stomach is shrunk with starvation,' John

suggested. 'I read somewhere that if people are dreadfully hungry, it's difficult for them to eat at first. When someone has been starving you shouldn't give them anything solid to eat to start with – just sips of sugary water.'

'We haven't got any water. And she's not starving because we gave her all that food yesterday. All our tea,' Mary said.

'It was only a few sandwiches. It wasn't much,' John said, rather indignantly. He was feeling hungry himself and thought longingly of the boiled egg that he had slipped into his pocket when Aunt Mabel's back was turned, even though he had eaten a second helping of porridge to make up for it.

'What are we going to do?' Ben said. 'It's freezing cold up here.'

It *was* cold. There was no sun today and the attic looked very bleak and bare. Outside, the sky looked thick and felted like an army blanket and the seagulls, wheeling, were like chips of snow against the grey.

'Let's light a fire,' John said. 'There's wood shavings in the cellar and we could get some sticks out of the garden.'

'Do you think we should?' Mary said solemnly. 'The chimney might catch fire or something.'

The boys regarded her with disgust.

'We'll see to the fire,' John said with a superior look. 'You and Victoria can clean up the attic and find the rugs and cushions. That's women's work.'

Mary went downstairs rather reluctantly. She was a little shy of Victoria who was so much older than she was – indeed, except when they had been playing hide-and-seek yesterday, she hadn't seemed to Mary like a child at all. Mary didn't think that Victoria would enjoy furnishing the attic and at first it looked as if she was right.

Victoria turned her mouth down at the corners and said sullenly, 'Do you mean we've got to sweep up the floors and dust? That isn't *fun*. I hate housework.'

'I rather like it,' Mary said. 'We never did anything like that in Africa. I like making beds and washing up . . .'

'Well I don't,' Victoria said roughly. 'I've had to do too much of it. I . . .' She stopped suddenly.

Mary thought this was a little odd. Surely they didn't make you do housework at boarding-school? She said quickly, 'You needn't help. It doesn't matter – it's only a game. We – we just thought you might like to.'

But Victoria followed her upstairs and after Mary had been sweeping with the dustpan and brush for a little, she said abruptly, 'I'll do that – I'll be quicker than you.'

She was quicker. She was very quick and neat, like Aunt Mabel. When the floor was clean, she shook the dirt out of the attic window and said cheerfully, 'Well – what do we do now?'

'We've got to find rugs and cushions.' Mary remembered that even if Victoria was a sort of refugee, she was still taking refuge in her own house, so she added, politely, 'If you don't mind, I mean.'

Victoria laughed. 'Why should *I* care? I might as well be hanged for a sheep as a lamb.'

And, in fact, she collected far more things than Mary would have dared to do – bright, silken cushions from one of the bedrooms and three gaily patterned, woollen rugs. When they staggered upstairs with their burdens, the boys had already lit the fire. The wood shavings were roaring up the chimney and John had found a stack of old, tarry road blocks in the cellar. They crackled and spat and made a delicious smell. Victoria spread a rug in front of the fire and knelt on it, her hands spread out to the flames. 'Isn't it warm and lovely?' she said.

Ben knelt beside her. 'Your hands are so thin I can see the fire through them,' he said.

'Don't be rude, Ben,' John said, but Victoria only smiled.

'He's not rude. He's a dear. I wish he was *my* brother.' She put an arm round Ben and hugged him tight, then went rather pink and scrambled to her feet. 'I know what we want,' she said. 'There's a brass fender downstairs. It's beautifully shiny and it'll look lovely with the fire dancing in it.'

They went downstairs – it would take all four of them to carry the fender, Victoria said – and as they reached the hall, they heard something that made them freeze in their tracks.

Someone was walking up the steps to the front door. Someone was putting the key in the lock. Victoria made a low, strangled sound and fled back up the stairs. Stiff with horror, the others stayed where they were. John had turned very white.

'*Hide*,' Ben said. He seized John's hand and dragged him into the dining room. There was a big sofa in the window, covered with a dust sheet. Quicker than it takes to tell, Ben – who was always good in emergencies – whipped up a corner of the dust sheet and scrambled underneath, pulling John with him.

Mary thought she would hide behind the sofa, but it was too late. The front door opened with a loud, sudden noise as if it had stuck fast through being shut for so long. Mary ran behind the open dining room door, and pulled it against her.

Someone came into the hall – or, rather, two people did, because one of them spoke to the other.

A man's voice said, 'It's probably a tramp, Mr Reynolds. Everyone in Henstable knows the house is shut up – a tramp might easily have decided to break in and hole up for the bad weather. He could've been here for ages, no one 'ud know. I suppose he got to thinking he was safe and lit a fire.'

Mary shuddered behind the door. *Of course*. When they lit the fire, they hadn't thought of the smoke!

The other man, who must be Mr Reynolds, Mary thought,

horrified, said, 'Surely Mrs Clark's been in? She would have known if there had been anyone here.' He had a cracked, old voice. The other man's was deeper and rougher.

'She's been off sick. Hurt her back, her husband said. She'll not have been in for a month or two.'

'Taking advantage of my absence. That's much more likely. You can't rely on anyone nowadays.' Mr Reynolds sounded furious and Mary thought it was rather horrid of him not to be sorry because Mrs Clark had hurt her back. 'All right, Jackson,' he said in a tired, irritable way, 'we'll have a look around.'

Their steps came along the hall and stopped. Mary realized that they were standing in the doorway of the dining room, very close to her, on the other side of the door. She held her breath and huddled back against the wall, trying to make herself as small as possible. They were so close that she could hear them breathing.

Mr Reynolds said, 'Good Lord, Jackson – look at this. Your tramp, or whoever he is, has been making himself at home, hasn't he? Eating off my Sheraton table ...' His voice rose in an angry squeak. 'My Dresden plate ...'

'Not broken, is it, Sir?' Jackson said. His voice was respectful and soothing.

'No. But it might have been. Heaven knows what else we shall find. I suppose we'd better see what damage has been done – then I shall have to get to the insurance people and the police.'

Mary shook behind the door. She shook so hard that she thought that they must hear her knees knocking together. What were John and Ben feeling like, under the dust cover? Surely, if the men looked at the sofa they would be bound to see them; even if the boys were lying quite flat and still, their shapes must show. And suppose they sneezed?

'In fact,' Mr Reynolds said, 'I think we'd better get on to the police first. I'll wait here, Jackson, and you go straight down to the station and come back with a constable. Several. Don't let them put you off – the police are much too casual about private property. Tell them *my house* has been broken into and a great deal of damage done. I want the culprit arrested.'

He sounded in a tearing rage and Mary clenched her fists. It would be dreadfully undignified to be caught by a policeman. She was frightened, but she was also angry because Mr Reynolds had said a lot of damage had been done when they had been so careful and worked so hard to make the neglected attic look nice. She came out from behind the door and said, 'There isn't any tramp, Mr Reynolds. There's only us.'

She saw a tall young man in a uniform like a chauffeur's, carrying an enormous fur rug over one arm. And standing in front of him was a little old man with a thick black coat buttoned up to his chin and a black hat pulled down over his forehead so that it almost seemed to rest on a thin, hooked nose like an eagle's beak. He stared and stared at Mary with a pair of glittering, angry eyes that seemed to be boring right through her. She could think of nothing to say so she just stood miserably twisting a piece of her skirt between her fingers.

'Who the devil are you?' he said, at last. 'Are you alone?'

There was a scuffling sound from the sofa, the sheet heaved and John appeared, very red in the face. He sneezed, because of the dust, and Ben, scrambling after him, sneezed too.

'Good Lord,' Mr Reynolds said. His bright eyes stared and his skinny beak of a nose flushed scarlet. 'Brats,' he said to the tall young man. 'Just a parcel of brats.' He wheeled round to Mary. 'What do you think you're doing here? No

– don't bother to tell me. The police will deal with you. The country's in a fine state when a man can't leave his house without it being broken into by a pack of delinquent brats.'

'Don't excite yourself, Mr Reynolds,' Jackson said in a soothing voice, but the old man took no notice of him. He was breathing hard and his eyes were bulging with fury.

'We're not delin . . . whatever you said,' Mary said loudly. 'We come from the house next door.'

'Oh. You come from the house next door. That makes you respectable, does it?' he said in a very nasty voice. 'Well, *I* don't think it does. What have you been doing here?'

'Just playing,' Mary said.

'*Playing?* Among all my valuable things?'

'We just played up in the attic,' John said. 'We thought it was all right because nobody seemed to have used it for ages and ages, and some of Aunt Mabel's things were still there. We haven't done any damage, really we haven't. We knew we had to be careful because of your pictures and things – we just borrowed a rug to put in front of the fire . . .' John stopped and went very pale. Mary and Ben, who were looking at him, knew why. Mary felt sick inside. She had forgotten the broken Bust.

'*Fire*,' Mr Reynolds said explosively. His nose flushed red again and the blue veins stood out on his forehead. 'D'you hear that, Jackson? They might have burned the house down. Fetch the police *at once*. Heaven knows what they've done. Breaking and entering – a parcel of thieving brats.'

'We're not thieves,' John said indignantly.

'Then what are you doing here?' His sharp eyes swept over the three of them and fixed on Ben. 'What have you got there? *In your hand*.'

Ben held out the green horse that he had taken out of his pocket when he was hiding under the dust cover. He had been stroking it for comfort. Mr Reynolds pounced on him, like a hawk on a mouse, and snatched it out of his hand.

He held it up triumphantly. 'Not thieves, eh?' he said with a grim, pleased smile. 'Then what are you doing with this? This piece of jade? You stole it, you little thief, took it out of my collection upstairs . . .'

'I didn't steal it, it's *mine*. I know it looks like some of your old things, but it's not. It was given to me . . .' Ben was quite as angry as Mr Reynolds. His skin was white and damp and his eyes shone dangerously.

'That's a fine story,' Mr Reynolds said, and made a curious, snorting noise through his nose. 'Who on earth would give a boy a valuable piece like this?' He had put on a pair of gold-rimmed spectacles and was examining the little horse and fondling it gently, as if he loved it.

'Miss Pin did.' Ben looked as if he was going to burst. 'I think you're very *rude*,' he said.

Mary gave a little gasp. But though Mr Reynolds went on frowning, his nose wasn't quite as red as it had been and a ghost of a smile touched his thin mouth.

'We'll see about that, won't we?' he said, quite pleasantly. Then his face went dark purple and he shouted, 'Jackson – take these children down to the station. I want them charged with breaking and entering. I am going upstairs to examine my collection of jade. I want to present the Inspector with a full list of what is missing.'

He turned on his heel and marched out of the dining room.

Mary ran after him and caught his arm. 'Please – please, Mr Reynolds, don't send us to the police. Just – just go upstairs and look in the cabinet and you'll *see* nothing's missing. The horse belongs to Ben, it really does, it's called Pin and it isn't precious like your things, it's . . .'

Mr Reynolds said nothing at all. He just shook her hand contemptuously off his arm and went on, up the stairs.

Jackson said softly behind her, 'Don't make him angrier. It won't do you a mite of good.' Mary turned round, her eyes brimming with tears and he added, quite gently, 'He can't tell if anything's missing just by *looking*. He's got so much stuff, see. He'll have to go right through all his insurance lists, it's the only way he can tell. And that'll take him hours and hours, I reckon.' He sighed heavily. 'In the meantime – I'm afraid I'll have to do as he says. Whatever got into you, breaking into a house like this? Does your mother know anything about it?'

'Our mother is dead,' Ben said in a cold, still voice.

'Oh,' Jackson said. 'Oh,' and looked at all three of them with a troubled expression.

John said suddenly, 'Before we go, can I go upstairs? I – I want to go to the bathroom.'

Jackson hesitated. 'All right. But be quiet – don't let him hear you. And quick. I'll give you three minutes. You needn't try to make a dash for it. I'm hanging on to these two.'

He took hold of Mary and Ben just above the elbow and held them in a firm, but not ungentle grip.

John sped up the stairs, running on the balls of his feet. Three minutes wasn't long, but it must be long enough to persuade Victoria to come down and tell her grandfather she was here. It might not make him any less angry, but if she told him they hadn't stolen anything, it might stop him sending them to the police station. She wouldn't be too frightened to do that, surely? Even if Mr Reynolds was a terrifying person – and he *was* – he was still her grandfather.

Victoria was crouching on the bed, all huddled up against

the wall. She had her head down on the beautiful shawl and her shoulders were shaking.

John said, 'Stop crying. You *must*. It's important.'

She sat up and looked at him, her face puffy with tears. 'Does he know – does he know I'm here?'

John shook his head. 'No. But . . .'

She said quickly, 'You won't tell him, will you?'

John fidgeted uneasily from one foot to the other. '*I* won't. But you've got to tell him.' Then the words came tumbling out of him very fast. 'He's dreadfully angry – he's going to send us down to the police station – he thinks we're thieves and robbers. And they'll send for Aunt Mabel and she'll be awfully upset and our father will too, and they may send us to prison for years and years – so you've got to come down and tell him we aren't thieves and that Ben didn't steal his little horse . . .'

'I can't,' she breathed, very low. Her eyes gazed at him; they were like deep, dark wells.

John gave a long, shaky sigh. 'You must, you know. He can't hurt you – even if he is cross. If you tell him everything – all about how horrid they were to you at school, he'll understand and take you away.'

She shook her head, looking frightened and mulish at one and the same time and John felt suddenly hot and red with anger. She didn't care about him and Mary and Ben, she didn't care if they were sent to prison for life. He couldn't believe that anyone could be so selfish and mean. He rushed across the attic and dragged her across the bed, shouting, 'You've *got* to come. You're just a stupid coward. It's stupid and silly to be frightened of *your grandfather*.'

She fought him like a mad person, pummelling his chest and scratching his face. Though she was taller and older, John was the heavier of the two and he had dragged her almost to the door of the attic when she gasped in a strangled voice, 'He's not – he's not my grandfather. Oh – you've broken my locket.'

The locket fell to the floor as John let go of her. He bent to pick it up. She had hurt him quite badly, his cheek was bleeding where she had scratched him, but he was far too curious to be angry. 'What do you mean?' he said, astonished. 'You *told* us . . .'

'I know.' She bit her lower lip and her eyes looked wild and scared – like a frightened wild animal's, John thought. She said slowly, 'I only meant – he's not my *real* grandfather.' She paused, bowing her head so that her dark hair fell forward and almost hid her face. Finally she mumbled in a low, rapid voice, 'My parents weren't my real parents either. My real mother abandoned me – she left me on the steps of the church, Mrs Clark says, and *they* adopted me. My father was Mr Reynolds' son and Mr Reynolds didn't want him to adopt a strange child – he wanted a grandson who was his own flesh and blood to inherit all his art treasures. So when my parents died he didn't want to look after me – he sent me off to a horrible boarding-school because he didn't want to see me – I think he almost *hates* me . . .'

Her eyes weren't wild now, but soft and dreamy. 'Who's Mrs Clark?' John asked, but he didn't wait for her answer because he was looking at the little gold locket that had broken open when it fell to the floor. Inside it, there was a picture. A picture just like the one in the photograph album, of Aunt Mabel when she was young.

'This isn't your locket,' he said, 'It's –'

But she wouldn't let him finish. 'It is mine – it *is*,' she said passionately. 'It . . . it was round my neck when I was found. I was dressed in beautiful clothes – all silk and lace – that's how I've always known my real parents must have been rich people, and I was wearing this locket. I – I think it must be my mother's picture . . .'

John looked at her wonderingly. Something very exciting and strange had happened and he could hardly believe it. Although he had always been sure, whatever Mary said, that queer and marvellous things *did* happen, it was always hard to believe it when they did.

'Oh . . . oh . . .' he started to say, 'oh, *Victoria* . . .'

He had no time to say any more, because there were loud, clumping steps on the stairs and Jackson appeared in the doorway of the attic. He looked very angry and bothered.

'There you are,' he said. His eyes went past John, to Victoria, and opened wide in surprise. 'Oh ho,' he said, and regarded John grimly. 'So that's what you were up to, was it? Sneaking off to warn your chum here. I suppose I might have known it. And I was fool enough to think you were just a pack of scared kids! I was even soft enough to feel a bit sorry for you . . .'

His face was scarlet with indignation. He took hold of John by the shoulder. 'Come on you,' he said to Victoria, and gave John a rough little push. 'And step lively. I shan't let any of you out of my sight till we're safe at the police station.'

9. Locked Up in the Police Station

The big, shiny car purred through the streets of Henstable with the four children huddled in the back, not speaking. Mary felt very miserable and scared – and hungry, too, because it was lunch time. She sat next to John and held his hand to comfort him though, in fact, John looked more thoughtful than frightened. His face was pink and his eyes were bright – almost, Mary thought, surprised, as if something extraordinarily nice and exciting had happened. He certainly didn't look like a criminal being taken to the police station.

Neither did Ben. He sat stolidly, his hands clenched on his knees. He had not spoken once and he was so furiously angry that his eyes were like hard, dark little stones. Mary knew he was angry about Pin and was glad of it; as long as he was angry he couldn't be scared, though he probably wouldn't have been scared anyway. He was too young, she thought, to understand the dreadful thing that was happening to them.

Victoria was frightened, though. She was crouching in the corner and shivering as if she was very cold. Her face looked just as it had when they first met her; a screwed up, pale, sullen face, glowering out of the window.

The car stopped. Jackson got out, opened the back door and jerked his head. 'Out,' he said curtly.

They went up some stone steps into a big, bare room where there was a kind of counter and a policeman standing behind it. The children waited while Jackson spoke to the policeman in a low voice. The policeman was a tall, red-faced man with a great deal of hair; not only did he have a vast, ginger moustache, but there were spikes of red hair growing stiffly out of his ears. He looked at the children while Jackson was talking and after a bit, he beckoned to them.

They went up to the counter. It was so high that Ben could barely see over it. The policeman spoke to them. They would have to stay here for a while, he said; they were to tell him their names and addresses and their parents would be sent for.

Ben's mouth was shut tight as a clamp and John seemed speechless – not through fear, exactly, it was more as if he was far away in a world of his own. Mary glanced at Victoria because she was so obviously the oldest, but she was clasping her arms across her chest and quivering and staring at the floor.

So it was Mary who talked to the policeman. She said that their name was Mallory, she told him where they lived and Aunt Mabel's telephone number. The policeman put little questions, to encourage her; though his voice was gruff it was also quite kind and after a little Mary began to feel a good deal less frightened. When she had finished, she glanced at Victoria again and suddenly realized what John had realized earlier: that Victoria only had to say she was Victoria Reynolds and everyone would know that they weren't criminals, only rather naughty children who had broken into someone else's house. And though her grandfather might still be very angry, he would hardly send his grand-daughter's friends to prison.

She was rather surprised because Victoria didn't speak up and say who she was, but she wasn't angry. Mary had a very kind heart and was always ready to make allowances for people: she thought Victoria was silly not to tell the policeman her name but she was very sorry for her, because she looked so pale and terrified.

Perhaps the policeman was sorry for her too because he

didn't question her, though he looked at her once or twice in a curious sort of way. Or perhaps he thought that she was a Mallory too.

When he had written down all the things that Mary told him, he took them behind the counter and into another room, where there was a bench and some chairs. It was a high, bleak room with a lot of bright, scrubbed, yellow paint and a small, barred window high up in one wall. The policeman said they were to wait there for a little while. Just after he had left, another policeman – a very young one – came in with a tray on which there were four steaming cups of tea that he put down on the bench. He didn't say anything but winked at them in a cheerful way.

In spite of his wink and the tea – which was so strong and sweet none of them could drink it – the next half hour was a very unhappy time. In fact it seemed more like half a day than half an hour. None of them spoke much. Ben just said, in a quiet, ominous voice, 'Just wait till Miss Pin hears of this!' and relapsed into a dark, gloomy silence. Victoria just sat and shook and John peered sideways at her from time to time – an odd, secretive glance that would have puzzled Mary, if she hadn't been so busy wondering what would happen to them. And what Aunt Mabel would say!

Perhaps even when they discovered who Victoria was, and that they hadn't stolen anything, they would still be sent to prison! Perhaps breaking into a house – Breaking and Entering, was what Mr Reynolds had said – was just as bad as stealing something. And they had broken the Bust. Perhaps once Mr Reynolds discovered that, they would all be thrown into jail straightaway, and not let out until they were quite old . . .

This thought was so alarming that she quite stopped worrying about how upset and angry Aunt Mabel was going to be, and when, finally, the door opened and Aunt Mabel was ushered in by the hairy policeman, Mary ran up to her, crying, 'Please – oh, please Aunt Mabel, don't let them send us to prison.'

Aunt Mabel's eyes were red and her face was pinched and cross, but she held Mary's head tightly against her side and said soothingly, 'There, there, my lamb, don't cry . . .' Then, as if she was rather ashamed of herself for being so kind and gentle, she pushed Mary away and said coldly, 'I am deeply ashamed – so ashamed I don't know what to say. Your Father will have to know – everyone will know. It will be in all the papers, you will have to come up before a magistrate . . .'

Ben pushed Mary aside and stood in front of Aunt Mabel. He burst out,' He said we were *thieves*. And we're not. Miss Pin knows. I'm going to tell her.'

His face was so set and burning with rage that John and Mary would have laughed, if it had not been such a solemn occasion. Then he ran towards the door, butted the hairy policeman in the stomach and squeezed past him. He took everyone by surprise; he was out of the police station and in the street, almost before the policeman could turn round.

'Ben,' Aunt Mabel called in a high voice, 'Ben, come back here . . .'

She would have gone after him if the policeman had not stopped her with a loud, good-natured laugh. 'Let him go, Mrs Haggard. We know where he lives, don't we? We can get hold of him when we want to.' And he went out, closing the door.

Aunt Mabel said, 'Well, you've got yourselves into a pretty pickle . . . You . . .' Then she saw Victoria, and her eyes sharpened with surprise.

John gave a queer little squeak of excitement. 'Aunt Mabel,' he said, 'this is Victoria. She is your Long Lost Daughter.'

Aunt Mabel looked thunderstruck. John said, 'I knew, because of the locket. She was wearing it when she was found on the steps of the church.' He beamed at Aunt Mabel, very proud and happy, as if he had quite forgotten he was locked in a police station. 'We went into the House of Secrets and we found the brass bedstead and the chest with your things in it and the picture of your baby that was stolen – and then we found Victoria had the locket with your picture in it . . .'

In a minute, he thought, when Aunt Mabel had taken in this wonderful news, she would open her arms wide and clasp Victoria to her bosom. He was a little surprised – even though perhaps he hadn't explained it very well – when Aunt Mabel did not do this. She simply stood there, her mouth opening and shutting, like a fish gasping for air.

Mary stammered, 'But . . . but I thought Mr Reynolds was her grandfather . . .'

'Only her *adopted* grandfather,' John explained. 'That's not the same thing at all.' He looked at Aunt Mabel solicitously. 'I suppose it's an awful shock. Would you feel better if you sat down?'

But Aunt Mabel wasn't just shocked. Something was dreadfully wrong. Her face had gone a curious, mottled colour as she looked at Victoria and suddenly she burst out, 'Why, *Vicky Clark*. What have you been telling them – you *wicked* girl?'

Victoria burst into tears.

'I couldn't help it, I couldn't . . .' she sobbed. 'They found me in the house and I was so scared . . . they kept asking questions on and on and they thought Mr Reynolds was my grandfather and I said yes, he was, because I thought otherwise they'd tell on me and I'd get into awful trouble. Then, later on, when I found they hadn't any more business being there than I had . . . I couldn't, I couldn't . . .'

John stared at her. He couldn't believe it. Why should Victoria have told such dreadful lies?

He said indignantly, 'But you had that locket! You said . . .'

She looked at him miserably. 'I took the locket out of the chest in the attic. It was so pretty, I only wanted to wear it for a little while. But – but I thought you'd think I'd stolen it. And – and anyway I'd been pretending to myself about it being my mother's locket . . .'

'But why did you tell us the other things? Do you mean it wasn't true, *none* of it – about the awful school and being adopted and your mother and father dying and everything . . .'

John was dreadfully angry. It was partly disappointment, of course – it had been so exciting and wonderful to think he had discovered Aunt Mabel's daughter – but he was also an upright boy who despised people who didn't tell the truth.

Victoria drew a long, sobbing breath. 'I didn't – I didn't mean to tell lies, but I just started and I went on. And it was nice thinking that I lived in that lovely house and that my real parents were rich and everything. It was sort of exciting and everything's really so horrible and *dull* . . .'

Aunt Mabel's voice was unexpectedly gentle. 'It wasn't all lies, John. Vicky's parents are dead. She's an orphan and she lives with her foster mother, Mrs Clark. Mrs Clark works for Mr Reynolds – she keeps the house clean for him when he's away.'

But John's face stayed cold and stony. He said, 'So that's how you had a key. You just came in and out through the back door. I think you're a nasty, lying little sneak. Telling us all those stories and making us sorry for you . . . and . . . eating our food . . .'

'I didn't want it,' Victoria shouted fiercely – she wasn't

crying now, but just as angry as John. 'D'you think I wanted that horrible, cold egg and that horrible bread and butter all covered with *dirt*? It's your fault – you made me eat it, you *made* me ...'

She looked thoroughly bad-tempered and cross but Mary felt, suddenly, rather sorry for her. It was their fault in a way, they'd wanted her to be mysterious and exciting. And it was silly of John to be angry when all Victoria had done was to pretend to be someone else – and John himself was always pretending. But of course, though it was all right to pretend, it was wrong to tell lies; sometimes it was very difficult to tell which you were doing.

Mary said, 'You should have told us. I mean, it was all right to pretend in the beginning, but after we'd been found out – when Mr Reynolds had caught us, I mean – you could have told us in the car, or something ...'

Victoria gave a sniff. 'I thought you'd hate me for telling those lies and think I was horrible, the way everyone else does. And I wanted us to be friends.'

'But we *were* friends,' Mary said, surprised. 'So you could have told us. And you should have told us you'd only borrowed the locket because ...'

Her voice trailed away. She had suddenly realized how awful it must be for Aunt Mabel when she came into the room and John said, 'this is your Long Lost Daughter', when it was only a girl she knew called Vicky Clark.

She looked at Aunt Mabel anxiously, but Aunt Mabel didn't appear in the least upset. She looked grim. She gave Mary an I'll-talk-to-you-later look. But when she turned to Victoria, her expression wasn't grim at all. It was kind and pitying.

She said, 'What were *you* doing in the house, Vicky? Did Mrs Clark know you were there?'

'Once she did,' Victoria said unhappily. 'She hurt her

back, see, about two months ago, and she said I was to go in and dust downstairs so the place would keep clean for Mr Reynolds. He's ever such a fussy man. Mrs Clark said I was to go home after school and give the little ones their tea and put them to bed and then go along to Mr Reynolds' house and clean. I didn't want to go – I was scared because the house was shut-up and spooky – but she said I was stupid. So I went and dusted like she said – the dining room and the stairs and the hall and then I was tired and my legs ached and I thought Mr Reynolds wouldn't mind if I sat down for a little while. So I went into that room and saw the piano . . .'

Aunt Mabel said softly, 'And then? What happened then?'

Victoria looked into Aunt Mabel's face and gave a relaxed little sigh, as if something she saw there made her feel soothed and comforted. She said, 'I played it. It's a lovely piano, it's got a lovely tone. And I wanted – I wanted to play it more than anything in the world. I *needed* to practise. The lady next door to Mrs Clark's used to let me practise on her piano and then she got a television set and she couldn't be bothered with me any more because they wanted to watch the television . . . though Mrs Clark said it was because she didn't like me, she said I looked so sour and cross no one *could* like me. And she said it wasn't worth my having music lessons any more if I couldn't practise.' She paused. 'I didn't hurt the piano. I didn't do any damage.'

'I'm sure you didn't,' Aunt Mabel said.

She was looking at Victoria in an odd way, almost as if she wanted to cry, and Victoria looked back at her with a sad, trusting expression on her face and said piteously, 'Will Mrs Clark have to know? About the police and everything? I did an awful thing, you see, I gave her back the front door key but I took the key out of the back door so I could get in to play the piano without anyone knowing. I didn't do anything else except once or twice I went to sleep on the bed in the attic because I was tired – I took an alarm clock so I'd wake up before it was dark. And now Mrs Clark'll find out and she'll send me back to the orphanage.' Her voice broke in a sob. 'I don't like Mrs Clark, but I don't want to go back to the orphanage.'

Aunt Mabel took a handkerchief out of her pocket and blew her nose. She said, 'I'm afraid Mrs Clark will have to know, unless Mr Reynolds decides to drop the charge. But he is a very hard and difficult man.'

She stared straight in front of her for a minute, as if she was thinking very hard. Then she did something that was quite unlike anything the children had ever seen her do. She went up to Victoria and put her arms round her and held her head tight against her shoulder. She said, 'Don't worry, Vicky dear. I'll try and think what is the best thing to do. You can come home with us and have something to eat and before you go home I'll see Mrs Clark and try to explain to her.'

'*Can* we go home?' John asked in an astonished voice. 'I thought we were going to be locked up.'

Aunt Mabel said dryly, 'No, John. Not that you don't deserve it. But in England, no one can be imprisoned without trial.'

John sighed deeply, with relief. And Victoria clung to Aunt Mabel, just as if she *had* been her long lost daughter, and cried a little.

10. 'I Want My Dad to Come Home'

When they got home, Ben was waiting on the doorstep. Before Aunt Mabel had closed the door, he said in an excited voice, 'There's a man come to see Miss Pin. He's talking to her in her room.'

'Talking to Miss *Pin*?' Aunt Mabel said. 'Whoever ...?'

'Miss Pin says he's her Man of Affairs,' Ben said importantly. 'And he wants to see you, Aunt Mabel.'

'What?' Aunt Mabel frowned. 'I suppose I'd better go and see what Miss Pin has been up to. Mary – go down to the kitchen and lay the table for tea.'

'*Tea*,' John said indignantly. 'But we haven't had lunch yet.'

'People who get arrested by the police must expect to miss their meals,' Aunt Mabel said, and walked down the passage to Miss Pin's room.

The children went down to the kitchen. 'My stomach's empty,' John said. 'It feels like a *drum*. What's in the larder, Mary?'

'There's a lovely big bowl of dripping.' Mary picked it up carefully and put it on the table, with the bread and the knife.

John sighed. 'I feel more like steak. Still, I suppose we're lucky not to be locked up in a cold cell and fed on dry crusts and water.'

'We may be yet,' Mary said gloomily. 'You heard what Aunt Mabel said. We'll have to come up before a magistrate. *He* may send us to prison.'

'No he won't,' Ben said suddenly. 'He'll send Mr Reynolds to prison. For stealing my horse.'

'He didn't steal it,' John said. 'Stealing is when you come stealthily, by night. He just took it because he thought it was his.'

'Well it wasn't,' Ben said. 'And he'd no right to take it. Miss Pin said so. She says she'll see I get it back.'

'*She* can't do anything,' John said. 'She's only an old woman. And just stop *talking* about your old horse. There are a lot of more important things to think about, like going to prison and dying of hunger.' He took the knife and began to cut thick slices of bread.

Ben looked miserable and angry at the same time.

'Never mind, Ben,' Mary said. 'I expect you'll get Pin back, in the end. I mean – when Mr Reynolds has had a good *look* at it, he'll see it isn't one of his. All his horses are terribly *valuable*.'

Ben said nothing. He just glared at John in a furious, smouldering way and tucked into the thick slice of bread and dripping Mary gave him. In spite of the prospect of prison, all their appetites were remarkably sound. Even Victoria, who had not said a word since they left the police station, had eaten her second slice of bread and dripping by the time Aunt Mabel came into the kitchen and closed the door behind her.

She had a puzzled look on her face. She said, in a hurried voice, 'Ben, come here. I have something to say to you.'

Ben gulped down his mouthful of bread and went up to her. She looked searchingly into his face. 'Ben – what have you said to Miss Pin?'

Ben shuffled his feet and stared at the floor. 'Nothing,' he said.

Aunt Mabel said quickly, 'I didn't mean you'd said anything wrong, Ben, you're too young to understand. But did you tell her I was poor?'

Ben went brick red. 'I did in a way. She *asked* me, see? I

wanted some money to buy something and she said couldn't you give it to me and I said, no, you couldn't. And she said she'd give me some money and she did, but it wasn't real money, only an old foreign coin.'

'Will you show me the coin, Ben?' Aunt Mabel said, and Ben fumbled in his pocket and brought out the little, bright yellow coin and gave it to her. She looked at it, turned it over and looked at it again. There was an odd, bemused expression on her face as if something had happened that she didn't understand at all. She said nothing for several minutes.

Then Mary said nervously, 'Is anything the matter, Aunt Mabel? Has anything happened? What has Ben done?'

Aunt Mabel looked at her as if from a great distance. 'There's someone upstairs who wants to talk to Ben,' she said.

She looked so vague, so flustered, so almost alarmed, that the children were afraid to ask any more questions. Ben stood still while Aunt Mabel scrubbed at his mouth with a corner of her apron and tried, rather unsuccessfully, to sleek back his tousled hair with a comb. The others followed and clustered in the doorway, feeling rather odd inside.

On one of the tables there were a great many papers, all spread out, and several thick-looking files. Behind the table sat a sharp-featured, rather dry-looking gentleman with a bald head and spectacles.

He looked at Ben.

'Is this the boy?' he asked in a cold voice. He took his spectacles off, put them on top of the papers and gave them a little flip – all without taking his eyes off Ben. They were chilly, grey eyes, the same colour as the English sea, and they regarded Ben with stern disapproval.

'Yes, Mr Green,' Aunt Mabel said. 'This is Ben. Benjamin Mallory.'

'Come here, Benjamin,' Mr Green said. 'Here – on the other side of the table.'

Ben glanced at Aunt Mabel who gave him a little push. He walked steadily up to the table and stood, very straight and still.

Mr Green looked at Aunt Mabel. 'What have you told him?'

'Nothing,' Aunt Mabel said.

Mr Green sighed and looked even more cold and disapproving.

'Very well, Mrs Haggard. Now Benjamin, I want you to listen to me very carefully. I'm a solicitor. Miss Pin's solicitor. Do you know what a solicitor is?'

'No,' Ben said.

'Well – oh, never mind. Now – you know Miss Pin, don't you?'

Ben looked at him boldly. 'Of course I do. She's my friend.'

Mr Green gave his spectacles another little flip. 'Your *friend*?' he said, giving the word a nasty, sarcastic sound. 'Do you really expect me to believe that? You're only a little boy. How can an old lady be your *friend*?'

Ben said loudly, 'She *is* my friend. Not my best friend, because Thomas is that, but my second best friend.'

Mr Green leaned back in his chair and twirled his spectacles in his hand. He said, incredulously, 'Do you mean that you like talking to her . . . that sort of thing?'

'We don't just talk,' Ben said. 'We play draughts. And she tells me stories. I like playing draughts and listening to stories.'

'She's a very old lady,' Mr Green said. 'I shouldn't have thought a boy would have been interested in anything such a very old lady had to say.'

This was such a very stupid remark that Ben did not bother to reply to it.

Mr Green settled his spectacles back on his thin, long nose and gazed at Ben thoughtfully for a moment. Then he said, 'I'm going to ask you a question, young man, and I want you to answer me quite truthfully. I shall know if you tell me a lie. Did anyone *tell* you to go and see Miss Pin and play draughts with her? Has your Aunt, for example, ever said that it would be a good thing if you got friendly with Miss Pin and were nice to her?'

Ben opened his mouth to answer but Aunt Mabel put in quickly, 'Mr Green, I cannot believe it is necessary to take this attitude. The child has *never* been encouraged to visit Miss Pin. It has been entirely his own doing.'

Mr Green sat up straight in his chair. He said in a weary voice, 'Mrs Haggard, that may or may not be true. I am simply trying to get at the truth in order to avoid trouble in the future. Miss Pin's relations . . .'

'Have never bothered with her,' Aunt Mabel said sharply.

'No doubt. But should she . . . should anything happen to her,' he went on with a quick glance at the watching children, 'I daresay they *will* bother. They may even contest the Will in the courts and try to prove that you had persuaded the boy to make friends with her for your own gain . . .'

The children did not understand. They stared at Mr Green and then at Aunt Mabel. Aunt Mabel's face was pale and nervous but Ben's was pale and angry.

He said furiously, 'No one asked me to be friends with Miss Pin. I just wanted to be because I *like* her. She can't help being old. And she tells lovely stories. If you don't believe that, you must be a stupid, horrible man . . .'

This was dreadfully rude and John and Mary gasped, but

Mr Green did not seem to mind at all. He even produced a smile – very small and rather sour, but still a smile.

He said, 'I believe you, Benjamin. I am very glad you are fond of Miss Pin, because she is very, very fond of you. So fond, in fact, that she has decided to give you a lot of money ...'

'But she hasn't got any,' Ben said. 'She *says* she has, I mean – she *thinks* she has ...' He felt hot and uncomfortable. It seemed very unkind to Miss Pin to tell this stiff, cold man that she didn't understand about real money. On the other hand, it might be even more unkind *not* to tell him. He might be terribly angry with Miss Pin for telling him stories and wasting his time. So he said, breathlessly, 'You see, she has a story she tells – about her Papa and his Enemies and the Treasure he left her to look after. B-but it's just a sort of game – the treasure is only a lot of foreign coins that you can't spend in England. She doesn't know that because it's a long time since she went to the shops but *I* know, because she gave me one. Look ...'

He put his lucky coin down on the table and watched Mr Green as he picked it up and looked at it. Ben said anxiously, 'You won't be angry with Miss Pin, will you? For ... for wasting your time and things ...'

Mr Green's thin mouth twitched violently. Mary and John had the impression – which couldn't be true, of course, because he was such a cold, humourless man – that he was trying very hard not to burst out laughing. He didn't laugh, though. He said, gently, 'This isn't a foreign coin, Ben. It isn't legal tender, either – that means you couldn't change it in a sweet shop. But it's real English money, all the same. It's a Golden Sovereign – I don't imagine you've ever seen one before.' He fondled the little coin tenderly and then handed it back to Ben. He went on slowly, 'Miss Pin *is* rich, Ben. I know she gets a little muddled sometimes, because she's old and falls asleep easily and dreams a lot – but she's not muddled about that. She is a very, very rich old lady and one day, Ben, you will be a very, very rich man ...'

Aunt Mabel said in a low voice, 'I don't think there is any need to go into that ...'

'No,' Mr Green said. 'No, perhaps not.' He drummed his fingers on the table top and cleared his throat. 'Well. Apart from her Will, Miss Pin has instructed me to deal with all her financial affairs. The jade is not to be sold for the moment but the sovereigns will cover all her current expenses, including,' – he smiled at Aunt Mabel – 'the very considerable amount she clearly owes you for all the years you have cared for her.'

Aunt Mabel said, in a funny, gasping voice, 'And to think I thought she hadn't a penny. When all the time she was sitting on a gold mine.'

'A gold mine?' John said, surprised.

Aunt Mabel smiled. 'Well – not quite. I meant her jade collection. Mr Green says it's worth a lot of money.'

'Priceless,' Mr Green said, lovingly.

Aunt Mabel sighed. 'All that old junk. Junk. That's what I thought it was. Can you imagine?'

Mr Green gave a short, dry laugh. 'Do you know, Mrs Haggard, there are pieces in that trunk that have not even been unpacked!'

'Incredible!' Aunt Mabel said.

Ben said suddenly, 'Do you mean my horse is really precious?'

Both Aunt Mabel and Mr Green looked at him in surprise. It was as if they had been so busy exclaiming over Miss Pin's fortune, that they had forgotten the children's presence.

'What horse?' Mr Green said.

'The one Mr Reynolds took. He shouldn't have taken it, Miss Pin gave it to me, he's a *thief*,' Ben said.

'And he said *we* were,' Mary burst out.

'Mr Reynolds – what has Mr Reynolds to do with it?' Mr Green said.

The children all started to talk at once but Mr Green held up his hand and said in a commanding voice, 'One at a time, please.' So Mary told him, rather hesitantly, about the House of Secrets and how Mr Reynolds had found them and taken Ben's horse and said they were a parcel of thieving brats and sent them down to the police station.

When she had finished, Mr Green said nothing for a few minutes except, 'Hmmm,' and played with his spectacles. Then he said, 'Well . . .' and looked at them all so gravely that they began to feel very guilty and scared. He put his spectacles on and looked at John over the top of the lenses. 'Tell me,' he said, 'you broke into this house – in itself, a very wrong thing to do, of course – but did you do any wilful damage? Did you break anything?'

John drew a deep, quivering breath and looked at Mary. There was no hope for it – they would have to explain about the broken Bust. But just as he was gathering his courage, Ben said loudly,

'I suppose if my horse really *is* precious, Miss Pin had better have him back. When Mr Reynolds gives him back to me, I mean. I don't suppose she knew he was really precious, do you? She wouldn't have given a really precious thing to a boy.'

His face was very sad. Mr Green looked at Aunt Mabel and smiled. Then he said, 'I think you can keep your horse, Ben. Miss Pin would like you to, I'm sure. In fact she would like you to have other things. Is there anything you want?'

Ben stared at him blankly.

'Come on, don't be shy. You're a young man of substance now,' Mr Green said jokingly. 'There must be something you'd like. Toys, books – anything you want.'

Ben's eyes grew large and dark and shiny. 'I want my Dad to come home,' he said

11. 'You Can Do What You Like to Me'

'Hmm,' Mr Green said. He stopped smiling and looked at Ben in a sad, rather sorry way.

And Ben went dreadfully white, as if he was going to faint.

'I feel sick,' he muttered, and clasped his hands over his stomach.

'Not on my good carpet,' Aunt Mabel said. She flew to him and led him, groaning, from the room.

'Excitement, I daresay,' Mr Green said. He stood up, thoughtfully tapping his teeth with one end of his spectacles. Then he folded them up, snapped them away into a red leather case and began to gather his papers together. 'I imagine your Aunt will be fully occupied for a little while. Perhaps you would convey my sympathies to Master Benjamin and tell Mrs Haggard I will contact her in the morning. I have a little business to do.' His mouth was set in a grimly amused smile, as if the little business was something he rather expected to enjoy.

The children waited while he fastened his briefcase and picked up his neat bowler hat and his neat, black umbrella. Then they showed him politely to the door. When he was gone, they stood in the hall and looked at each other. John and Mary felt rather confused and their stomachs had that queer, fluttery feeling stomachs have when you are in the middle of something exciting.

John said thoughtfully, 'I think I could do with some more bread-and-dripping,' and set off purposefully towards the kitchen. Mary followed him and, after a minute, Victoria followed her; lagging behind and moving very quietly as if she wasn't sure whether she was wanted or not.

Their minds were so full of what had happened that they ate several slices of bread-and-dripping without speaking. Then, when his stomach was feeling slightly distended, but more comfortable, John wiped his mouth with the back of his hand and said, 'I don't think Ben really understands. Not about Wills and things.'

'Perhaps we'd better not tell him,' Mary said. 'It would upset him dreadfully. Not being rich, I mean, but thinking that Miss Pin might die one day. He'd simply hate to think of her dying.' A lump came into her own throat and her eyes smarted.

John said, 'Do you think he'll turn into a fat, rich man like that fat man on the plane from Nairobi? Do you remember – the one who kept on drinking whisky and smoking simply enormous cigars?'

Mary giggled. 'Perhaps Ben'll be so rich that he'll buy an aeroplane of his own.'

'And a yacht and a car – a marvellous, exotic car, like a Golden Hawk.'

They began to laugh. It seemed so absurd to think of little Ben, grown very fat and riding round in a huge car, drinking whisky and smoking cigars. They laughed, a bit hysterically, until their sides and their stomachs ached: everything they said made them laugh harder. 'Perhaps he'll wear a *bowler hat*,' John gasped, and the idea of Ben in a bowler hat was one of the funniest things they had ever heard. They reeled about the room, half doubled over and clutching at each other for support.

They might have gone on for ages, giggling in that wild, silly way, if Victoria had not made an odd, choking sound. That sobered them. They stopped cavorting round the room and looked at her, wiping their streaming eyes.

She was standing by the kitchen door, hunched up and miserable, and trying very hard not to cry.

'What's up?' John said. For a moment he felt rather irritated; it seemed that Victoria was always crying, or about to cry. Then he remembered what had happened in the police station and thought that perhaps she had rather a lot to cry about. So he said awkwardly, 'I'm sorry. I'm sorry I was so cross and beastly.'

Victoria rubbed her eyes with her knuckles. 'It's all right,' she said. 'It's just – just that you're so *lucky*. Whatever happens – whatever the police do, your Aunt'll see nothing very awful happens. Everything turns out all right for you. Nothing does for me – you'll see, I shall just get into dreadful trouble and Mrs Clark'll send me back to the orphanage and I shan't be able to play the piano again, ever, *ever* . . .' And two tears spilled out of her eyes and rolled down her cheeks, fat and pale as pearls.

'You mind about not playing the piano dreadfully, don't you?' Mary said slowly. This was something that was rather hard for her to understand.

'More than anything,' Victoria said in a hard, sad little voice. 'More than anything in the whole world.'

John and Mary looked at her, troubled. 'Is Mrs Clark horrid to you?' John asked.

Victoria shrugged her shoulders. 'Oh – she's not so bad. Not really. But I have to do such a lot of things. I get up early and do the fires and dress the children and then I have a lot of housework to do when I come home from school.' She bit her lip. 'I wouldn't mind that, but she doesn't like me. Nor does anyone. I lived with four foster mothers before I came to Mrs Clark and none of them liked me.' She looked at Mary. 'I bet you don't know what that's like. Always having people not like you.'

Mary thought that it must be very strange and sad. It had

been bad enough when they had first come to Henstable and she had thought that Aunt Mabel didn't like them. And Aunt Mabel had been the only person who had ever not liked her – only one person, in her whole life! She thought that it would be sure to make you cross and unhappy if people didn't like you.

She said, 'We like you. Me and John and Ben.'

'Do you?' Victoria said. 'Do you, really?'

'Yes,' John said sturdily. 'But *you* don't like many people, do you? And it's jolly hard for people to like you, if you don't like *them*.'

'I suppose it is,' Victoria said. She looked very wistful and solemn, as if she was thinking very hard. Then she said, 'I suppose if you start to like people, they start to like *you*. I think, even the *idea* of liking someone makes me feel nicer inside. And I do like some people now. I like you two, and Ben. And . . . and I *love* your Aunt Mabel.'

Her face lit up as she said this and John and Mary were quite surprised. They hadn't expected anyone else to see that Aunt Mabel was so much nicer than she seemed to be.

Then, suddenly, the door bell rang, very loud and long as if someone very important was standing on the steps and could not bear to be kept waiting, even for a minute. They heard Aunt Mabel come quickly down the stairs and along the passage to open the door. Then they heard a voice. A cracked, high, old man's voice.

'It's Mr Reynolds,' Mary whispered. She clutched John's hand very tight. They listened. They could hear Mr Reynolds saying something and Aunt Mabel answering him, but they couldn't hear what either of them said. Then their voices died right away – they must have gone into the dining room, John thought – but the children still stood, still and strained and listening.

They stood there for about ten minutes. Then they heard

the voices again. And Aunt Mabel called, 'Children. John, Mary – come up here.'

John went up the stairs, very slowly and reluctantly, dragging his feet. Mary followed. Her heart was beating so fast that it felt like flapping wings, trapped in her throat.

Mr Reynolds was alone. He was standing in the hall, hunched in his thick, black coat and looking like a very old, fierce bird. He was looking round him with his sharp, bright eyes as if he was reckoning up how much the carpet and the pictures were worth. As the children came into the hall, Aunt Mabel walked down the stairs carrying Ben who was wearing John's dressing gown and looked a yellowish, greenish colour.

Mr Reynolds was frowning. His nose was purple and there were fat veins standing out on his forehead. *He's found out about the Bust*, John thought and stood, frozen, waiting for the terrible outburst of anger that was bound to come.

But to his surprise – to his utter astonishment – Mr Reynolds cleared his throat and said, 'I have come to apologize to you all. You had no right – no right at all – to break into my house, but it was wrong of me to jump to the conclusions I did. I wish to apologize for calling you thieves and, by implication, liars, and especially, I want to apologize to this young gentleman here.'

He made a stiff, formal bow towards Ben who was sitting on the stairs, glowering at him.

It was a remarkably handsome apology. The children let out shaky little breaths of relief.

Mr Reynolds took something out of his pocket and held it on his open palm. It was the green horse. 'This isn't mine,' he said. 'Though to be fair to myself, I think my mistake understandable. This is a very good piece and I have one almost exactly like it.'

'It's a lot prettier than any of yours,' Ben said firmly.

Mr Reynolds went on frowning, but his nose was a lot less flushed and red. 'I hope you will look after it, then,' he said. He paused, as if he was thinking of something. 'I suppose,' he said slowly, 'I suppose you wouldn't like to ask your Aunt if you could sell it to me?'

'No,' Ben said. 'It was given to me by my friend, Miss Pin.' He stood up shakily, his legs feeling very wobbly beneath him, came down the stairs and held out his hand.

Mr Reynolds sighed. He looked at Ben closely and then gave him the horse – but reluctantly, as if he were sorry to part with it. Then he sighed again and said, 'Well, that's settled, I hope. No hard feelings.' He smiled at them all, looking almost benign. 'I shall speak to the police and tell them to drop the charge against you. You have been very naughty children, but as far as I can see, you have done no damage ...'

Mary gasped. It was such a loud gasp that Mr Reynolds stopped speaking and everyone turned to look at her.

'What's the matter, Mary?' Aunt Mabel asked.

'I expect she's going to be sick too,' Ben said hopefully.

Mary shook her head. She looked straight at Mr Reynolds and said in a faint voice, 'It's very kind of you, to apologize and that. But ... but we *did* break something. I'm sorry. It was an accident. I ... I knocked into it and it fell over.' When she had got it out, she felt horribly frightened, but relieved underneath.

'*What* fell over?' Mr Reynolds said in an awful voice. He wasn't looking benign any more.

'Come and see,' Ben said. He took hold of Mr Reynolds' coat sleeve – just as if he was an ordinary old man and not terrifying at all – and tugged at it. He said, over his shoulder, 'I shan't catch cold, Aunt Mabel. I've got my slippers on.'

Aunt Mabel seemed too stunned to protest. She just shook

her head in a bewildered way and opened the front door. The curious little procession, Ben in his dressing gown, Aunt Mabel in her apron, Mr Reynolds and John and Mary, went down the steps of *The Haven* and along the pavement.

Victoria followed them. But when they went into the House of Secrets, she stayed outside. She was quivering and her eyes were wide and dark; suddenly a sly look came into them and she took to her heels and ran.

'See?' Ben said proudly. 'We put another one in its place. I think this one is nicer. It's mine, but you can have it because we broke your one.'

'And who gave you *this*, may I ask?' Mr Reynolds said in a sarcastic tone. 'If I may say so, young man, you seem to have some extraordinary benefactors.' He took out a pair of gold-rimmed spectacles and looked up at the head of the African boy.

'Well,' he said after a minute. 'Well . . .' His sharp, angry old face seemed to soften; he looked surprised and almost awed. 'This is a remarkably fine piece of work.' He looked at Ben and said, not sarcastically at all, but quite humbly, 'Would you mind telling me who gave it to you?'

'Nobody. I bought it,' Ben said. 'I put a deposit down on it. Uncle Abe made it – he's a sculptor. But he's not very good at selling the things he makes, so he said as I was a friend I could have it, cheap.'

'How much?' Mr Reynolds snapped – not angrily, but eagerly.

'Seventy-five pounds,' Ben said promptly. 'I put down a deposit of one and three halfpence.'

'Indeed?' Mr Reynolds took his spectacles off and polished them on a beautiful, white handkerchief. 'And he's not selling very much at the moment, you say?' His eyes had a new, sharp glint in them. 'I think I'd like to have a talk to your Uncle Abe . . .'

'He's . . .' Aunt Mabel began but she got no further because the front door, which had been left ajar, burst open suddenly and Victoria marched into the hall.

She was breathing very fast as if she had been running hard and there were bright spots of colour in her cheeks. She said, quickly, 'You mustn't be angry with Mary because she didn't do it. She said she did because I was so scared, but she didn't. I did. I was going to run away but then I thought about what they said about liking people, so I came back.' She flung her head back and stood, very proud and straight. 'You can do what you like to me,' she said.

Mr Reynolds stammered, 'What do you mean? Who – who *is* this?'

He turned helplessly to Aunt Mabel, who was smiling.

'This is Victoria Clark,' she said in a curiously cheerful voice. 'I told you about her.'

'Oh. Oh – yes.' As he looked at Victoria, Mr Reynolds' eyes were sharp but kind. 'So you're the girl who likes to play the piano,' he said at last.

Victoria looked back at him. It had taken a lot of courage to come back and say she had broken the Bust but she was not a naturally brave person, and was beginning to feel very weak and trembly. She whispered, so low he could hardly hear, 'I'm sorry. I wasn't doing any harm. It's a lovely piano. I didn't bang at the keys or anything . . .'

John broke in, 'She had to play with the soft pedal down all the time so she couldn't do the bit with trumpets blowing.'

'Trumpets blowing?' Mr Reynolds said. He looked interested. He said gently to Victoria, 'Perhaps you'd like to come and play it to me now. Loud as you like . . .'

Victoria was white to the lips. 'No . . . no, I couldn't,' she murmured.

Aunt Mabel said briskly, 'Nonsense, child. It's only fair. You've been using Mr Reynolds' piano without his permission. He's got a right to hear how well you played on it.'

Victoria gave a little, gasping sigh. 'Now?'

'No time like the present,' Aunt Mabel said. 'John – take Ben home. He should be in bed.'

'I feel all right,' Ben said. 'Just empty but that's natural. I lost my bread-and-dripping *and* my breakfast and yesterday's supper too, I should think . . .'

'That'll do,' Aunt Mabel said. 'Clear off – the pair of you.'

She turned to Victoria and her voice was quite different – gentle and coaxing. 'Come along, dear,' she said.

She put her hand on Victoria's shoulder and Victoria walked towards the piano room, like a girl in a dream.

The big room looked quite different with the heavy curtains drawn back and the window open letting in the garden smells of earth and wet grass. The sunlight slanted across the piano where Victoria sat, playing for Mr Reynolds. She played some of the pieces of music she had played for the Mallory children and then some others that Mary had not heard. Her face was grave, but relaxed and calm.

After a little, Mr Reynolds who was sitting on the sofa with Aunt Mabel, began to whisper. Mary, standing behind them so Aunt Mabel shouldn't see her and send her home with John and Ben, could hear what he said.

'It's incredible – do you really mean she hasn't been properly taught?'

'Only a local music teacher,' Aunt Mabel murmured. 'And that has stopped. Apparently she's not allowed lessons any more.'

'Scandalous,' Mr Reynolds said. As he turned sideways, Mary could see that his thin nose had flushed purple again. 'Disgraceful. I shall speak to Mrs Clark. It's wicked to neglect a talent like this.'

Aunt Mabel sighed a little. 'I don't think it will be easy to make Mrs Clark understand,' she said. 'She's a very good sort of woman and I'm sure she does her best, but I've heard in the town that the girl's not easy.'

'Brilliant people never are,' Mr Reynolds said. 'D'you mean the girl's not cared for properly?'

His voice had risen. Victoria played a loud chord on the piano and then sat still and scowling. She said, 'I can't play if you talk.'

'Vicky,' Aunt Mabel said reproachfully, but Mr Reynolds laughed, his cackly laugh, and stood up.

'Quite right,' he said. 'She needs a bit of temperament if she's to get on.' He went over to the piano and stood looking down at Victoria and stroking his chin. She went on scowling at him but he did not seem to mind. He said abruptly, 'What school do you go to?'

Victoria said, 'It doesn't matter, does it? I'm leaving at the end of next term when I'm fifteen. I'm going into a shop.'

'A *shop*.' The veins bulged out on Mr Reynolds' forehead until they looked as if they might burst through the skin. He glared at Victoria and then walked to the far end of the room, mumbling fiercely to himself. He swung round on his heel. 'Nonsense,' he said loudly. 'Utter nonsense.' He glared at Victoria again. 'Tell me – how would you like to have lessons – go to a proper music school?'

Victoria looked at him, her lips parted. Her eyes were big and glowing. Then she closed her mouth into an ugly, hard line and looked down at her lap. 'Mrs Clark wouldn't let me.'

'Mrs Clark. *Mrs Clark?* What right has she to stop you?'

'She looks after me,' Victoria said.

'That's no reason, no reason at all. I'll speak to her – make some financial arrangement.' He frowned severely, thinking aloud. 'A bit of local tuition first, then the Royal Academy – perhaps Berlin. I know an excellent man . . .'

'Mr Reynolds,' Aunt Mabel said in a warning voice. He started and looked at her as if he had forgotten she was there. 'You can't collect people like . . . like pictures,' Aunt Mabel went on. 'Victoria has a lot of talent, but you can't just buy her and put her in your collection.'

'What . . . what . . .' Mr Reynolds was staring at Aunt Mabel as if no one had ever spoken to him like that before.

Aunt Mabel's colour heightened a little and she clasped her hands tightly in her lap. 'She's young,' she said. 'She has to be looked after. It would be very kind of you to pay for her to have lessons, but there are other things to be considered . . .'

'Mrs Clark wouldn't let me,' Victoria said in a loud, dull voice. 'And even if she did, there's just the kitchen and one living room with all the kids banging about and shouting. So even if I could have lessons, there's nowhere for me to practise. And if I can't practise I won't be *good*, and if I can't be good – famous like Myra Hess – I'd rather not play at all.'

Mr Reynolds chuckled in an approving sort of way. 'That's the right attitude.' He looked thoughtfully at Victoria, 'Are you happy with Mrs Clark – fond of her, that sort of thing?'

Victoria said nothing.

'I want the truth,' Mr Reynolds said impatiently. 'Don't say "yes" just because you think it's unkind to say "no".'

Mary thought this was very sensible of him; it showed that he understood how someone might feel.

Victoria took a deep breath. 'No,' she said. 'I'm not fond of her and she doesn't like me and I'm not happy there.'

'Then I see no reason why you should remain there,' Mr Reynolds said. 'Do you, Mrs Haggard?' And he shot Aunt Mabel a sly, twinkling glance.

Mary could keep silent no longer. The most wonderful idea had been churning round and round inside her all the time she had been standing quiet, and out of sight and listening. She ran up to Aunt Mabel, scarlet with excitement, and said, 'She could come and live with *us* and she could come and practise *here* and you'd be able to afford it now because Miss Pin is rich after all and Uncle Abe may be able to sell his statues so *he'll* be rich and you will, too, won't you, with two lodgers who *pay* ...'

Aunt Mabel raised her eyebrows. 'Who told you they didn't?' She started to smile but then seemed to remember something, and stopped. 'It seems to me that you know more than is good for you,' she said.

12. The Best Thing of All

'But what did Uncle Abe say?' John asked, almost irritably.

It had been a most exciting day but too much excitement is like over-eating; it leaves you feeling liverish. Besides, John had missed some of the things that had happened towards the end – the best things, it seemed to him. While Victoria played to Mr Reynolds *he* had been sent home with Ben, and Ben had been sick again. And then, when Aunt Mabel took Victoria home and left John and Mary to eat supper alone with strict instructions to go to bed immediately afterwards, Uncle Abe had lumbered upstairs to have what he called a 'very private conversation with my Agent and Benefactor'. That was Ben. So it was no wonder John was feeling left out and a little cross.

Ben was sitting up in bed, his face the ivory colour of piano keys, but his eyes were bright and dancing with excitement.

'Mr Reynolds went to see him in his workshop – he's going to buy all the statues. Fat Woman Kneeling and all. Uncle Abe said it was a lucky break . . .'

Mary said, 'The House of Secrets has been awfully lucky, hasn't it? We ought to call it the Lucky House. Because if we hadn't broken that Bust we'd never have put Uncle Abe's thing there and Mr Reynolds would never have seen it and bought it.'

'He's not going to buy that one,' Ben said quickly. 'That one's mine.'

'But you can't keep it,' John said. 'Not if it's worth a lot of money.'

'Yes, I can,' Ben said in a lordly way. 'You know what Mr Green said. I can have anything I like.'

This was really insufferably cocky. John thought: he'll turn into a horrible person if he goes on like this.

But Ben wasn't as bad as he had sounded. 'I don't suppose I'll have enough to buy the African boy,' he said. 'But Uncle Abe said I can keep him. He said it was Commission – that's what Agents get. Because I sort of told Mr Reynolds about him – that's what Agents do.'

Downstairs, the front door banged. It was Aunt Mabel, coming home. She came upstairs and into their attic bedroom.

'What happened?' Mary asked, bouncing up and down on her bed in her vest and knickers, her face on fire with excitement. 'What did Mrs Clark say? Was she cross?'

'All in good time,' Aunt Mabel said. 'Get into your night things.'

When she first came in she had been smiling a faint, pleased smile but now it had faded and she watched them scramble into their pyjamas with a puzzled frown.

She said, after a little, 'There's something I want to ask you. Something I don't understand.' She cleared her throat as if it had an uncomfortable lump in it. 'It's not the sort of thing I should have expected from you children. I know I've sometimes thought, perhaps unfairly, that you were rather spoiled, but I've never – not once – thought you were unkind. And yet . . .' She swallowed hard as if the lump in her throat was still there.

'What have we done wrong?' Mary said unhappily. Aunt Mabel looked so stern and solemn – it seemed dreadful, after this splendid day.

Aunt Mabel looked at her searchingly. 'Don't you know? Or you, John?'

John and Mary shook their heads. Aunt Mabel looked at

their worried faces and seemed to hesitate for a moment. Then she sighed and said, 'I know it's fun to play jokes on people sometimes. But now and again jokes aren't funny – sometimes they can be very unkind. It is rather unkind, don't you think, when you know someone once had a little baby that they loved very much, to come marching in with a strange girl and pretend that this *is* the baby, grown up?'

Her hands were folded in front of her and Mary saw that she clasped them together very tightly, as if to stop them shaking.

She said, 'But Aunt Mabel, we thought Victoria was your girl. I mean, John did. He told you – it was because of the locket and because of what she said – we thought what she said was true, we didn't know it was just a game. And it *might* have been her, mightn't it? Victoria might have been your baby that was stolen by Enemies . . .'

'Stolen? Enemies?' Aunt Mabel said in an astonished voice. 'What do you mean?'

'Ben told us,' John said. 'After I'd found the photograph of the baby. Didn't you, Ben?'

'Miss Pin told *me*,' Ben said. 'She said it was dreadfully sad because you had lost your little girl and I said, did the Enemies steal her, and she said yes . . .'

Aunt Mabel started laughing. The children were rather shocked because it didn't seem anything to laugh about. But Aunt Mabel laughed until the tears came into her eyes. And then she cried for a little while, without laughing.

When she could speak, she said, 'Oh Ben – darling little Ben. I'm so sorry – of course none of you would have played such a trick on me! I don't understand about the Enemies, but I know what Miss Pin meant. My poor baby died, she was never very strong, and one morning after I'd put her in her pram, she just closed her eyes and went to sleep for . . . for ever.' Her mouth trembled a little but she went on firmly,

'So you see, I *did* lose her, though not quite in the way you thought . . .'

The children sat in their beds, very silent and solemn. This was very sad, much sadder than they had realized. Aunt Mabel seemed to know what they were thinking because she said softly, 'If someone you love dies, you know one thing – you know they're never going to be unhappy or in pain any more. It would have been much worse if my baby really *had* been lost, in the way you meant. Because I would never have known if she was happy or not, would I? She might have been living with people who didn't love her, perhaps, even, neglected her . . .' She stopped and drew in her breath sharply.

Mary said, in a hushed voice, 'Like Victoria?'

Aunt Mabel nodded. Her upper lip was caught between her teeth and she sat down, rather suddenly, on Mary's bed as if her legs felt shaky.

Mary came out from under the bedclothes and slid along to her. She said awkwardly, 'I'm sorry. It would have been so nice if Victoria had been your girl.'

'You mean it would have been like something in a story? I suppose it would have been exciting – though very unlikely.'

Mary shook her head. 'I didn't mean because of that. I meant it would have been nice for you. Because then you'd have had a family to . . . to *like*.'

Aunt Mabel stared at her. Then she coughed, rather violently, until her face was red, pulled Mary on to her lap and said in a funny, choking voice, 'You're all the family I want.'

She said nothing more for a minute, just rocked Mary backwards and forwards and watched John and Ben with eyes that were very bright and shining.

At last she said, 'Though I daresay I shall be able to

manage Victoria too.' And in a voice that was steadier now, she told them that she had talked to Mrs Clark who was quite willing – indeed, very glad – to give up being Victoria's foster mother. Though she didn't really dislike Victoria she had more than enough to do with her own children, especially since she had hurt her back and the only reason she hadn't sent Victoria back to the orphanage was that she thought the girl was so difficult and cross that no one else would be willing to look after her. 'So if they agree, and I expect they will,' Aunt Mabel said, 'I'll be her foster mother and she'll live here and Mr Reynolds will pay for her to have music lessons and let her practise on the piano next door until she is old enough to go wherever he wants to send her.' She looked at the children uncertainly, 'You won't mind? I mean you're quite fond of her, aren't you?'

'Oh,' Mary said. 'Oh – it'll be lovely. We'll be such a nice family, two girls and two boys . . .'

Aunt Mabel hugged and kissed Mary without speaking, then tipped her gently off her lap and went over to John and Ben and hugged and kissed over and over again, rather as if to make up for all the times she hadn't kissed them. In fact, John and Ben who didn't like being kissed all that much, thought she was overdoing it. John was beginning to wriggle when the telephone rang downstairs.

'I'll go,' he said and slid out of Aunt Mabel's arms and shot out of the door.

Aunt Mabel, her arms empty, looked hungrily at Ben, but he said quickly, 'I want a drink, I'm awfully dry.'

Aunt Mabel fetched him a glass of water from the bathroom but he had only had time to just sip at it when John burst into the room shouting, 'Oh – this is the best thing, the best thing of all. Do you know who that was? That was *Dad*.'

Immediately, there was pandemonium; so much noise in

the room and so many questions being asked that no one could hear what they were, let alone answer them. Finally, by dint of getting hold of John by the shoulders and shaking him quite hard, Aunt Mabel managed to get out of him that Mr Mallory was waiting on the telephone to speak to her.

'Goodness – and my hair's coming down,' she said in a flustered voice and ran out of the room, light as a girl.

'He can't see you on the telephone,' John shouted after her. Then he began to laugh – or perhaps 'crow' would be a better word because that is just what he sounded like, a fat, barn rooster, crowing. He jumped up and down, making this extraordinary noise, his face bright red and glistening.

'He's at the station,' he shouted, 'at the station, at the station. He wanted to telephone from the Airport but there wasn't time because he wanted to catch the last train. He'll be here any minute – any *second*.'

Mary began to cry, out of happiness. The tears rolled out of her eyes, down her cheeks and into her mouth, tasting warm and salt.

Ben got out of bed and stood on his head against the wall because he couldn't think of anything else to do.

'What do you think you're doing, young man?' Aunt Mabel said as she came back into the room. 'You'll be sick again, mark my words. A fine welcome for your father!'

She seized Ben by the seat of his pyjamas and jerked him right side up. 'Now,' she said in a commanding voice, 'be quiet – all of you.'

She waited while Mary's sobs quietened and John's crowing died down to a series of small, strangled hiccoughs.

Then she said, 'I want you to listen – we've only got a few minutes. Your father has been dreadfully ill. He went off into the bush, in a very wild part of Kenya, and caught a fever. He was lying in his tent, all alone, when a local tribesman found him and took him to hospital, but for weeks no one knew who he was – he didn't even seem to know himself. His memory came back a few days ago and he went straight to Nairobi to catch the first plane. He's better of course, but he's not strong, still – you mustn't bounce at him too much or shout too loud . . .'

Ben had been too busy thinking to listen. As soon as Aunt Mabel paused for breath, he said, 'Are we going back to Africa?'

'I don't know, dear,' Aunt Mabel said. 'You mustn't build on it. Your father may not be able to afford to take you.'

Ben drew a deep breath. '*I* can afford it,' he said grandly. 'I can afford anything I like. And if we don't go back to Africa, I shall pay to have Thomas flown over here, and Balthazar too, and if Dad wants to retire I shall buy him a television set, so he won't be bored, living in England.'

Aunt Mabel started to laugh but stopped herself. 'That's quite enough of that sort of talk, Ben,' she said crushingly. 'You're getting above yourself. Miss Pin may have made a fuss of you, she may even want to make you a few small presents but you must understand that you'll have what's good for you and no more. You're not a sort of little prince – you're just a little boy. And your nose needs wiping.'

She dived at him, handkerchief at the ready, but he danced out of her way.

Then the door bell rang; a piercing sound, bright as a sword.

John and Mary were out of the door in a flash but Ben lingered, just for a second. He had to have the last word.

'I'm not just a little boy,' he said, and drew himself up with dignity. 'Mr Green says I'm a Man of Substance.'

Also by Nina Bawden

THE PEPPERMINT PIG

Johnnie was just a little pig, but somehow his great naughtiness kept Poll and Theo cheerful through one of the most difficult years of their lives. (Winner of the 1976 Guardian Award.)

THE WITCH'S DAUGHTER

All the children were frightened of Perdita, until Tim and his blind sister, Janey, came from the mainland along with the sinister Mr Jones.

ON THE RUN

Eleven-year-old Ben has his hands full keeping his two friends safe from dangers at home – for one is the son of an African politician in exile and the other is on the run from the Welfare.

A HANDFUL OF THIEVES

When the sinister Mr Gribble disappears with Gran's savings, Fred and the other members of the Cemetery Committee decide to take on the dangerous and hair-raising task of tracking down the thief.

REBEL ON A ROCK

All they could see when they got out of the car was a great, grim rock sticking up out of a sea that seemed almost solid. So this was Polis, the end of their journey, the beautiful fortress city Albert had promised. 'Seems more like the end of the world to me,' Charlie said gloomily, and Jo agreed with him. She didn't know, then, that she was to be involved in matters of life and death.

THE FINDING

Alex doesn't know his birthday because he was found abandoned next to Cleopatra's Needle, so instead of a birthday he celebrates his Finding. After inheriting an unexpected fortune, Alex's life suddenly becomes very exciting indeed.

CARRIE'S WAR

The war rages, but Carrie, tucked away in a Welsh mining village, is more concerned with the rights and wrongs of the quarrel between her scrimping, miserable host, Councillor Evans, his mysterious, sad sister, and the wonderful, loving Hepzibah.

THE RUNAWAY SUMMER

Mary was unhappy most of the time because her parents were getting a divorce and had dumped her on Aunt Alice. But when she found herself worrying about someone else, her own problems seemed less.

SQUIB

'Squib's scared of you taking him home,' said Sammy. 'His auntie's a wicked witch, she ties him up in the laundry basket sometimes,' and Kate, who felt there was some fearful mystery, couldn't rest until she found out the truth.

THE WHITE HORSE GANG

Sam, Rose and Abe are the White Horse Gang. They hatch a shocking plot to kidnap a little boy – and then find out how hard it is to be as ruthless as proper kidnappers.

THE ROBBERS

When Philip has to decide whether to obey his father or to help Doug, his friend, he finds it the most difficult decision of his life.

KEPT IN THE DARK

Clara, Bosie and Noel found the big, strange, isolated house and the grandparents they'd never met rather daunting. But when David turned up and claimed he belonged there too, things became even more disturbing.

Some other Puffins

WOOF!

Allan Ahlberg

Eric had always wanted a dog so he was not unhappy when he found that he had turned into a dog one night, especially when he found that he was able to change back again quite quickly.

RACSO AND THE RATS OF NIMH

Leslie Jane Conly

A sequel to *Mrs Frisby and the Rats of NIMH* in which Mrs Frisby and her son Timothy help in the fight to save their valley from flooding.

THE PRIME MINISTER'S BRAIN

Gillian Cross

The fiendish hypnotizer, first encountered in *The Demon Head-master*, now plans to gain control of No. 10 Downing Street and lure the Prime Minister into his evil control.

COME BACK SOON

Judy Gardiner

Val is disturbed when her scatty mother walks out and leaves the family. She soon learns much about herself and her relationships.

JELLYBEAN

Tessa Duder

A gentle, modern novel about Geraldine, or 'Jellybean', a young girl growing up in a one-parent family.

SEASONS OF SPLENDOUR

Madhur Jaffrey

A beautiful introduction to India, lavishly illustrated by Michael Foreman, with anecdotes from the author's childhood preceding each retelling of these mythological tales from the Hindu epics.

ELEANOR, ELIZABETH

Libby Gleeson

Eleanor has been wary of her new home so far: the landscape is strange, the faces in the classroom unfriendly. Then, unexpectedly, Eleanor's lonely new life changes with the discovery of her grandmother's old diary. Now, with a bush fire rampaging just behind them, her life and the lives of Ken, Mike and six-year-old Billy depend on how she uses what she has learned about this alien world. She needs help, and only her grandmother, sixty-five years away, can give it to her.

A STITCH IN TIME

Penelope Lively

This seaside holiday is a time of finding things for Maria: names for birds and wild flowers, fossils in the Dorset rocks, a new friend, Martin, a different Maria who likes noisy games as well as sitting quietly thinking. And a little girl called Harriet who lived in this holiday house a hundred years ago, and sewed an elaborate sampler - but why didn't she finish it?

A PAIR OF JESUS-BOOTS

Sylvia Sherry

Liverpool-bred Rocky dreams of becoming a real crook like his big brother, but when he does get involved with criminals it is only his old sandals, or 'Jesus-boots', that save his life.